Snowflakes and Song Lyrics
A WILLIAMSVILLE INN STORY

HANK EDWARDS

STARTLED MONKEYS MEDIA

This is a work of fiction. Names, characters, businesses, places, events and incidents are either the products of the author's imagination or used in a fictitious manner. Any resemblance to actual persons, living or dead, or actual events is purely coincidental.

Snowflakes and Song Lyrics ©2019 Hank Edwards
Cover design by Brigham Vaughn
Book design and production by Hank Edwards
Editing by M. A. Hinkle

All rights reserved. This book or any portion thereof may not be reproduced or used in any manner whatsoever without the express written permission of the publisher except for the use of brief quotations in a book review.

Printed in the United States of America

First Publication, 2019

Summary:

When a shy and unsure guy jumps at the chance to anonymously help his favorite out singer write an original Christmas song, love can't be far behind.

Will Johnson is traveling for work the weeks before Christmas and staying in a small hotel in upstate New York. It's all pretty routine, until he discovers his window overlooks the courtyard patio of one of his favorite up and coming gay singers, Rex Garland. Even more amazing, Will overhears Rex's creative process as the singer struggles to write an original Christmas song.

When Will receives a flash of lyrical inspiration, he decides to share the lyrics with his idol in a secret note left on Rex's patio table. This sets off a chain of events that include coincidental meetings, more inspired lyrics, and a tiny snowman that just might capture Rex's heart and make this Christmas one neither of them will ever forget.

Snowflakes and Song Lyrics takes place in the Williamsville Inn series world, and is a funny, sweet and heartwarming celebrity and the boy-next-door tale which includes secret admirer notes and a classic love story.

Contents

Chapter 1	1
Chapter 2	16
Chapter 3	22
Chapter 4	28
Chapter 5	38
Chapter 6	43
Chapter 7	60
Chapter 8	65
Chapter 9	76
Chapter 10	87
Chapter 11	90
Chapter 12	101
Chapter 13	114
Epilogue	125
About the Author	135
Also by Hank Edwards	137

Chapter One

"You are like a sad little unicorn lost in a rural snowscape." Will snorted a laugh as he fought with his necktie. "You're not helping me focus on getting this damn thing tied."

"It's just so sad," Carter said with an elaborate sigh. "All of it makes me sad. Do you get off on the fact that your life makes me sad?"

Will dropped his gaze to where he had propped his phone up on the dresser beneath the mirror, angled so he and Carter could see each other in the video chat app. Carter wore a neon blue sweatband around his forehead, which pushed his thick, dark hair up into a veritable fountain on top of his head. He was currently making duck faces, and Will laughed.

"I can see you," Will said.

"I know. That's why I was doing it. So how long have you been sentenced to this place? Where is it again? The tundra?"

"It's not a sentence, and it's not the tundra," Will said, finally managing to get the tie knotted. He smiled and held his hands out. "There!" He turned to face the phone. "Tada!"

Carter inspected him with a critical eye. "The back of it is too long."

"What?" Will turned back to the mirror and saw the skinny tail hung just a bit longer than the front of the tie. "Dammit."

"Where'd you get that tie anyway?" Carter asked. "1992?"

Will loosened the tie and started all over again, grumbling, "I got it for Christmas last year, so it's not out of style."

"You're so cute," Carter said. "Apparently those two weeks we dated didn't have any impact on you at all."

"Oh, they had an impact," Will said.

Carter looked wounded. "Be nice."

Will grinned down at the phone as he worked on the tie. "You spoiled me for anyone else."

Carter beamed. "Smooth talker."

"Just speaking the truth, my friend."

"Well, right back at you," Carter said. "Things would be a lot simpler if we could have just figured out how to be a couple instead of a couple of friends."

"You know, I'm glad we realized it when we did," Will said. "You're my best friend. And now, when we go out to the bars, if a guy asks me if you're any good in bed, I can truthfully say that I've sampled your wares and that you are highly recommended."

"My wares?" Carter leaned in close to the phone and lowered his voice. "Are you speaking in code because you've been abducted by the local townspeople and need help?"

Will chuckled. "Nope." He finished up with the tie again and inspected it. "There. How's that?"

"Turn to me," Carter instructed, and Will turned toward the phone. "Hmm. Hands at your side, please."

"Just tell me if the tie looks—"

"Do it!" Carter snapped, and Will pressed his hands against his thighs. "Don't look so scared."

"I feel like a goat in front of a T-rex," Will said.

"You should be so lucky." Carter looked him up and down. "Smile."

Will smiled.

"Smile less like a serial killer at a rural truck stop."

Will laughed. "That was very specific."

"When you head out to the local truck stop to cruise men, you'll thank me for putting that idea in your head," Carter said. "Turn around."

"I really don't have time for—"

"Turn!"

Will did a quick turn.

"How about you slow it down a notch, Adam Rippon. This isn't the Nationals."

Will sighed and did a slow turn. When he faced the phone again, he raised his eyebrows. "Satisfied?"

Carter smiled. "I just wanted to see that fine ass again."

Will carried the phone into the bathroom and set it on the counter, propped against the mirror.

"I hope you're not going to make me watch you take a crap," Carter said.

"Gross," Will said. "And no. I'm brushing my teeth and combing my hair."

"You use a comb?"

"You know my morning routine," Will said. "Don't act like it's a surprise."

"You never really answered my question from before."

Will stuck his toothbrush in his mouth, saying around it, "What question?"

"How long you've been sentenced to that place," Carter said. "And what you're doing there. Also, where are you again? East of Nowhere, Nebraska?"

"Oh my God, you never listen to me," Will said around the minty foam in his mouth. "I'm in Williamsville, New York, not

Nebraska. It's a little south of Buffalo. At least, I think it's south."

"Not sure because they had a hood over your head during the car ride?" Carter asked.

Will laughed and sprayed toothpaste across the mirror. "Dammit, stop making me laugh."

Carter laughed, a clear, sparkling sound that never failed to make Will smile. "It's a gift. I don't own it. I can't believe you've been sentenced to, and I quote, 'a town maybe south of Buffalo, New York,' when it's this close to Christmas. Who am I going to take shopping? Who's going to sit on Santa's lap with me?" Carter pouted. "I don't like this new job of yours."

Will rinsed his mouth and checked his teeth in the mirror. "What about David?"

Carter rolled his eyes. "David is not Christmas cavorting material."

Will looked at the phone with a cocked eyebrow. "We cavort?"

Carter gave him a look filled with pity. "Oh, sweetie. You're not going to do well without me there, are you? Do they have any gay bars there so you don't lose your gay card?"

"Buffalo has some," Will said. "And it's not too far to drive."

"Buffalo? Hey, that sounds familiar." Carter picked up his phone. "I saw something about Buffalo last night."

"They getting a hundred feet of snow?" Will asked.

"Well, that, too, but something else. Dammit, what was it?"

Will checked his appearance in the mirror once more, then picked up the phone. "Thanks for chatting. You helped me feel less nervous about my first day here."

Carter smiled. "You're welcome. Just know that Boston is much drearier without you here."

"You'll find someone on Grindr to brighten up your days and nights, I'm sure," Will said with a smirk.

"I hope you find someone out there too," Carter said, then

smiled brightly. "Maybe you can enter that famous dogsled race they have!"

"That's the Iditarod, and it's in Alaska, not New York."

Carter frowned. "Did you just call me an idiot?"

Will smirked. "I am now. I need to go."

"Right. And do what again?"

"Kick off the process of transferring this branch's human resource records to a new system."

Carter made a face. "Ew."

"Yeah, I won't be very popular for a while," Will said. "And I gotta go."

"Have a good one," Carter said. "I'll find that news about Buffalo and send it along. Let me know how things go today."

"I will. Bye."

Will disconnected the call and slid the phone in his pocket. He crossed the hotel room and looked out the window. Down below lay a courtyard completely boxed in by the walls of the hotel, all of it covered in a bright white blanket of snow. Overhead, flat, gray cloud cover obscured the sun and sky. If the weather was going to be like this for the whole four weeks of his assignment, he might need to order a UV light online.

He packed up his laptop and some notebooks, grabbed his coat, and headed out the door.

❄

WILL STOOD IN THE AISLE OF THE SMALL CAFETERIA, between the sandwich counter and the salad bar. He looked between both options a few times. A salad would be best—he was carrying some extra weight—but a sandwich seemed more in order to celebrate completing the first half of his first day.

As he waited in line to give the sandwich maker his order,

Will's phone buzzed in his pocket. He looked at it and found a text from Carter.

How was the morning? Have you lost any toes to frostbite? I found what I wanted to tell you about Buffalo. Sharpen your stalker skills because your all-time favorite gay singer is performing in Buffalo: REX GARLAND!

A warm flush started in Will's chest and spread to his face. Rex Garland? He couldn't believe it. Rex Garland was going to be performing in Buffalo? A half-hour's drive away from the hotel? Holy shit. Why hadn't he seen a post about it? He followed Rex on every form of social media.

"What can I get you?"

Will looked up, his goofy grin slipping at the bored expression of the woman waiting to make his sandwich. "Oh, hi. Sorry, just got some good news on a text."

"Great. What'll you have?"

Will told her his order and looked back at his phone, bouncing between apps as he searched for some kind of post from Rex about being in Buffalo. There was nothing about it on Instagram or his Facebook page. Maybe in Twitter?

"Hey, happy-go-lucky newbie," the sandwich woman said. "Here."

He looked up and found her holding a to-go container out over the counter. Will apologized and took the container, then grabbed a bottle of water and headed for the checkout. Once he'd paid, he found a small table near the windows and sat down, ignoring his sandwich as he continued to investigate.

There it was, buried in Rex's Twitter stream. Will sucked in a breath as he read the short statement: *Rexaroos in Buffalo! I'll be performing at The Side-Eye all of December starting this Friday! Come on out and say hi!*

Rexaroos was the name Rex called his fan base, and Will couldn't stop grinning. Rex Garland, *the* Rex Garland, was going to be performing for the entire month just down the road. Maybe this work assignment wasn't so bad after all.

Still grinning, Will ate his sandwich as he opened a map app and found where The Side-Eye was located. He checked out the website and felt a giddy thrill when he saw the dance floor butting right up against the stage. Oh, if only he could find a spot right up front and be able to look up Rex's long, strong body to his trimmed dark beard, wide, white smile, and dark brown eyes. Maybe Rex would look right at Will as he sang his most famous song, the one that catapulted him into the gay community's consciousness: "Safe Inside Your Arms."

Oh, to have that moment with Rex. To have any moment with him.

It wasn't just Rex's looks, though, to be honest, the singer did hit all of Will's physical requirements. Will had noticed his handsome, strong torso covered with dark, trimmed hair and round, solid ass with an equally appealing bulge up front, but listening to Rex's lyrics had really cemented the attraction.

An attraction millions of other gay men felt as well. And most of those men were a lot better looking than Will. They were certainly not as overweight as Will.

Well, no need to get ahead of himself with all of this. He would just be happy to get a chance to see Rex perform live.

Will noticed the time and hurriedly finished eating his sandwich. It wouldn't look good for him to return late from lunch his first day.

❅

THE WILLIAMSVILLE INN HAD SEEN BETTER DAYS. Most likely sometime back in the 1960s. The early 1960s.

Will entered his room after a long first day on the job, and the heat nearly made him pass out in the entryway. It had to be ninety degrees! He desperately pulled off clothing as he searched for a thermostat, but by the time he was down to socks and his boxer briefs, he'd had no luck.

"So I've died and gone to Hell, and this is what I have to look forward to for eternity?" Will muttered.

The heating/air conditioning unit under the window—a long metal contraption with a number of vents set at an upward angle—made a thumping noise followed by a quiet hiss. Will sidestepped to the end of the bed and peered down at the thing. A stamp with the brand name Rest Easy was affixed to one corner, and warm air gusting out of the vents blew the sheer curtains away from the windowsill.

Will approached the unit and discovered a small metal flap on a hinge at one end. Underneath was a small knob with a faded line painted on it. The knob was turned all the way over to COOL, and Will sighed. No more cool setting to try, apparently.

"So much for resting easy, I guess."

He pulled the flimsy white curtains aside and inspected the window. Happiness filled him when he discovered the age of the hotel at last worked in his favor, and one side of the window was a slider he could open for some fresh air. The locking mechanism was old, however, and took some struggle before it finally released and allowed him to shove the window open with a squeal of the metal frames scraping together.

Will closed his eyes and drew in a deep breath of the fresh, cool air. He released it slowly and opened his eyes to look down into the courtyard. His room was on the top floor of the three-story building, and the first-floor rooms across from his all had small patios outside a sliding door. Metal café tables and chairs were provided for each room, and all of it was covered in snow. A quartet of lights in the style of old streetlamps, complete with large round frosted glass shades, provided gentle illumination to the area.

Just as he was wondering if the first-floor rooms cost more because of the tiny patios, one of the sliding doors almost directly across from his window opened, and a man stepped out.

He was tall, with dark hair and a matching full beard. A flannel shirt covered a white tee that hugged his broad chest and flat stomach. The cuffs of tight black jeans had been tucked into black Doc Martens. Something about the man seemed familiar, and Will guessed he'd seen him around the hotel. Someone like that would have definitely caught Will's eye.

But then the man turned to call to someone still inside the room, and the sound of his voice tripped recognition in Will's brain.

Rex Garland.

Will sucked in a breath and stared down into the courtyard, watching Rex pace around the cafe table, leaving a path in the snow. His hands were stuffed into the front pockets of his jeans, and he seemed to be muttering to himself.

A burning in his chest reminded Will to let out his breath and pull another one in.

Rex Garland was staying at his hotel. Would he be here for the entire run of his appearances at the Side-Eye? Will's heart pounded, and a fresh sheen of sweat covered his body. Even the bottoms of his feet were damp!

A man joined Rex out on the patio, and the two of them spoke in low tones. Will watched, lips slightly parted as he absently rubbed a hand through the fine hair covering his chest. He couldn't make out any words of their conversation until Rex threw his hands in the air and said, "I know I need to get it done, okay? Back the fuck off."

The other man held his hands up in a sign of surrender and went back inside the room.

Rex's paces around the small café table picked up speed, and

Will could hear him talking to himself. He hated to see his favorite singer in such a state.

Suddenly, Rex stopped and stared across the courtyard. Will pressed his forehead to the glass in an effort to see straight down, but he wasn't able to. When he looked back, he discovered Rex looking right up at his window. Realizing he must look pretty fucking creepy standing in front of his window in his underwear, Will dropped to the floor and lay there for a moment listening to the heating unit rattle and hiss.

Shit. Now what?

Will rolled onto his belly and did an Army crawl away from the window until he'd reached the far side of the bed. He got up and hurried into the bathroom where he sat on the lid of the toilet with his head in his hands.

Rex Garland was staying at his hotel.

Rex Garland was having a hard time with something and had shouted at one of his team.

Rex Garland had more than likely seen Will standing in his boxer briefs at the window and watching him.

Carter was going to love this story.

❄

"You have got to be fucking kidding me," Carter said.

"I can assure you, I'm not," Will said, giving the phone propped up on the desk a raised-eyebrows glance. "Rex Garland is staying in my hotel."

"*The* Rex Garland?" Carter narrowed his eyes. "You're sure it was him?"

Will gave him a stone-faced stare. "Honey, I know Rex Garland."

"Yeah, I'll give you that," Carter said. Then his face brightened. "Are you going to go knock on his door and fanboy all over him?"

"Um, that's going to be a hard no," Will said and quickly looked away from the phone back to his laptop, where he was trying to find the best route to take to get to The Side-Eye.

"You're acting funny."

"Hm? What?" Will pretended to be studying the same map he'd been looking at for several minutes.

"What happened? Something happened. Out with it."

Will sat back in the chair, hands on his head as he stared up at the ceiling and groaned. "I don't want to tell you!"

Carter gasped. "Oh my God, you did go to his room and fanboy all over him!" He made tsking sounds. "Oh, Big Willie."

"No, I did not do that," Will snapped. He took a breath and let it out before returning his gaze to the phone. "It's really hot in my room because the heating unit won't stop blowing."

"Sounds dirty," Carter said.

"Believe me when I tell you it is not, in any way, dirty," Will said. "That's why I'm wearing a T-shirt and boxer shorts right now. I called down to the desk, and they sent someone up who managed to get the heat down to something like eighty-two degrees, but..."

"You've got hot blood in you, and every degree above sixty-nine is like five degrees," Carter said in a monotone.

"I don't think I've ever been that specific with my temperature complaints," Will grumbled. "Did you just say that so you could say 'sixty-nine' aloud?"

"Maybe." Carter grinned. "Anyway, enough about me. Back to the hot maintenance man. Did you sixty-nine him?"

"Um, he was kind of gross, and, no, we did not engage in sixty-nine."

"Probably a good move on your part."

"Probably."

"So it's really hot in your room, so you....." Carter's expression went slack. "Were you standing at the window naked, and he saw you?"

"What? No!" Will shifted his gaze back to the laptop screen.

"Oh my God, you can't look at me," Carter nearly shrieked. "You *were* naked! He saw you naked? Did he look happy about it? I bet he loves bears. He seems like a bear lover to me. Did he whip it out and start masturbating right there on the spot like in a porn?"

Will thumped his head down on the desktop. "Oh my God. Please stop talking."

"You have to tell me what happened right this fucking minute before I explode!"

If only he would explode. That might save Will years of embarrassment as Carter brought the whole thing up over and over again.

"I wasn't naked," Will said without lifting his head.

"Really? Well, shoot."

Will picked up his head and looked at the phone. "I was in my underwear."

"Yes!" Carter danced around with the phone in his hand, giving Will a blurry view of his apartment living room. "It was a porn. I'm so happy right now I can't stop smiling. So did he come on his chest and then run his fingers through it and lick them clean?"

"Please stop talking," Will groused.

"Come on, give me the deets."

"The deets are as follows," Will said and held up his index finger. "One, my room will be overly warm for probably the length of my stay, and there are no other rooms available because half of them are booked into January and the other half are being remodeled."

"Too bad you couldn't have gotten a remodeled room, am I right?"

Will glared at him in silence.

Carter cleared his throat. "Sorry. Please continue with your countdown. Or count-up."

"Two." Will held up a second finger. "I have a window that opens to allow in cool, fresh air."

"Oh, that's a nice feature."

Will nodded. "I agree." He held up a third finger. "Three, I stripped down to my boxer briefs and stood in front of the open window to cool down. That's when I realized Rex Garland was in the first-floor room directly across from me. His room has a sliding door to a small patio, and he was out there talking with someone."

"How'd he look?"

"Rex?"

Carter made a face. "No, the stranger who was with him. Yes, Rex!"

Will smiled. "He looked good. Really, really good." His smile faded, and he cocked his head. "But he was upset about something the other guy was saying. I couldn't make out any of their conversation, but I heard Rex when he practically shouted something like, 'I know I have to get it done' or something like that."

"Huh, wonder what that was about," Carter said.

"Yeah, me too."

"So any more fingers you want to show me, or are you done now?"

Will fixed the phone with a scowl and held up another finger. "Four, Rex may have looked up at my window and possibly seen me standing in my underwear, but I can't be sure. Either way, I dropped down out of sight and crawled to the other side of the bed."

Carter pursed his lips and nodded. "Classy."

"Not my finest hour, I admit," Will said.

"Well, even if he did see you, I'm sure he'd never recognize you again, right?" Carter said.

Will nodded as a tiny flame of hope flickered in his chest. "Right. He was pretty far away."

"Maybe he didn't have his contacts in?" Carter suggested.

"Right!" Will said, feeling even better. "And who knows? Maybe the sun was reflecting off the window glass."

"There you go," Carter said. "That's the spirit."

A horrendous buzzing sound erupted on Carter's end of the call, making them both flinch.

"You still haven't gotten your door buzzer fixed?" Will asked.

"I'm on the list," Carter said, then waggled his eyebrows. "That's my Grindr date, baby."

Will smiled and shook his head. "You're incorrigible."

"Don't knock it till you try it."

"Be careful," Will said.

"Hey, it's me." Carter smiled. "You be careful out there in Montana."

Will sighed. "I'm in New York state."

"Same. Love you, William."

"Love you back, Carter. Text me later so I know you're okay."

"I'll send you all the gory details." The buzzer sounded again, and Carter rolled his eyes. "Ugh, he's so needy. Bye."

Will laughed and disconnected the call. He looked at the map to the Side-Eye bar some more, then closed his laptop. Tonight was definitely not the right night for him to go see Rex perform, but soon. He turned off the desk lamp, and darkness consumed the room. The only illumination was the glow from the courtyard lamps coming in through the sheer curtain.

Moving to the window, Will pushed aside the curtain and looked down at the sliding door to Rex's room. All the lights were off, and Will thought about one of Rex's songs titled "Lights Out, No One's Home."

The air coming in the open window was deliciously crisp, and Will breathed in deep. There was a hint of snow in the air, and he smiled. He really was a winter person. Carter liked to tease him about moving to the Arctic, but Will had always run a little hot. And now with the extra weight, he really could imagine living in the Great White North.

Now that he'd thought about Rex's song, the lyrics were running through his mind.

> *I've been knocking at the*
> *Door to your heart so long,*
> *And all I get in response is*
> *Lights out, no one's home.*

A walk to one of the nearby restaurants for dinner and listening to Rex's latest album through his headphones sounded like the perfect ending for this day. He left the window open and went about getting dressed, humming Rex's song.

Chapter Two

A couple of days later, Will entered the alcove in the hotel lobby where the breakfast bar was arranged. It was included in the price of his room, and the food was surprisingly better than Will had expected. He had started eating a big breakfast and taking a couple pieces of fruit to the office with him for lunch. The only problem with that setup was extreme hunger by the time he got back to the hotel.

There were a couple of other people meandering back and forth between the many offerings of the buffet, but Will ignored them. He didn't have the energy to meet anyone's eye until he'd had a cup of coffee. Meeting someone's gaze might mean an exchange of head nods or, even worse, spoken greetings.

He scooped scrambled eggs onto his plate and reached for the spoon to the hash browns. The man in front of him turned back and reached for the spoon at the same time, and his fingers closed around Will's hand, trapping both of them there holding the utensil.

"Oh, sorry," Will said, and tried to pull his hand away, but the man held tight.

"I guess since you're on the bottom that means you beat me to it."

The familiar deep voice brought Will's head up with a snap.

Rex Garland smiled at him. All the air left Will's lungs in a huff of disbelief, taking along his ability to think and any possible capacity of speech. He stared at Rex's handsome face, taking in the careful messiness of his dark hair, the neatly trimmed beard around full lips, and warm brown eyes with fine lines at the corners. White wireless headphones nestled in his ears, and Will wondered what Rex Garland listened to when he wasn't singing.

"Sorry, guess I should let you get your hashies," Rex said and released Will's hand.

Will thought he made a sound, something like, "Garmph," but he couldn't be sure. His hand seemed disconnected from his arm as it lifted the spoon and dropped a heap of hash browns on top of his eggs.

Rex lifted perfectly trimmed eyebrows as he looked at Will's plate.

"Going for the budget farmer's omelet, I see," Rex said.

"What?" Will couldn't look away from the man.

"Farmer's omelets have hash browns folded right inside," Rex said, then shrugged. "It was a stretch for a joke, since you have scrambled eggs and not an omelet." He widened his eyes, and his smile widened. "And I'm rambling because I haven't had coffee yet."

Will managed a breathless laugh that sounded more like a wheeze. "Yeah. Me too. Or neither. Me neither." He made a face and finally looked away. "Either?"

"Either?" Rex said, pronouncing it "eye-ther" and sending a blast of lust right to Will's groin.

"Let's call the whole thing off!" Will practically shouted.

A horrendously loud barrage of laughter burst out of him that sounded like a donkey in labor.

During a breech birth.

In an echo chamber.

He clamped his mouth shut as shame practically lit his face on fire.

"Sorry," Will whispered.

Rex chuckled. "No worries." He plopped some hash browns on top of the scrambled eggs on his own plate and winked. "Now you can tell everyone you started a trend. The budget farmer's omelet."

Will smiled and restrained himself from laughing. "Yeah. I'm trendy."

Rex looked him up and down with a smirk. "I can see that." He lifted a hand and turned his back, humming as he walked away and leaving Will standing speechless at the breakfast buffet.

What the hell just happened?

❆

WILL STILL HADN'T FULLY RECOVERED FROM HIS BREAKFAST run-in with Rex by the end of the day.

He couldn't bring himself to tell Carter about the interaction, not yet, anyway. Carter would completely ridicule Will for how he'd reacted, and Will wasn't yet ready to share that humiliation. Also, a small part of him wanted to savor the meeting for a time, keep it inside his chest like a delicious secret, even if he had acted like a babbling idiot.

The room was stifling when he walked in, and it made him gasp. The housekeeper, Doreen, must have closed the window after she'd cleaned his room. He hurried to the window and pushed it aside, letting in the beautifully cold air.

On his second day in the hotel, Will had rushed out of his room and nearly knocked over the housekeeping cart parked outside his door. Doreen had poked her head out of the room across the hall and apologized, and they shared a laugh before Will introduced himself and let her know he'd be staying there up to Christmas.

He'd have to remember to ask her to leave the window open when she was done.

The lamps in the empty courtyard illuminated the light snowfall, and Will smiled. Even if traffic would be in a snarl tomorrow morning, he did hope they got more snow soon.

He changed out of his work clothes and pulled up a restaurant app on his phone to pick a new place to eat. A rib joint had a number of positive reviews, and Will decided to give it a try. After one more look out his window—no sign of Rex—he ventured out.

The rib place was close by, and the food was amazing. When Will got back to the hotel, he typed the restaurant's name in a note-taking app on his phone. A brief consideration of driving to the Side-Eye to catch Rex's performance was quickly dismissed after a healthy burp and a swirl of snow against the screen of the window.

Will promised himself he'd get to the Side-Eye sometime soon as he stripped down to his underwear and stretched out on the bed. In minutes, he was asleep.

Sometime later, he awoke to singing. No, that wasn't right. It was more like someone playing guitar and practicing a song. Where was he?

Memory returned, and he popped his eyes open, wide awake as if hit by a bucket of cold water.

Rex Garland.

Holy hell, that voice. Though it was tainted with exasperation, the velvet timbre soothed Will's sleep-addled brain. The room was dimly lit by the lowest setting on the lamp farthest from the window. A frigid breeze gusted in the open window, making Will shiver in delight.

He got up and scrounged through the dresser drawers for a

pair of sleep pants and a T-shirt, then switched off the lamp. The courtyard lamps cast their gentle glow through the window, drawing Will closer.

"Heart filled with season..." An aggravated strum of strings followed by, "Fuck me."

Will's heart beat faster as he lowered himself into the desk chair by the window. He slowly leaned forward until he was able to peer down into the courtyard and see the patios across from him. Rex sat at the café table outside his room, guitar in hand and head bowed down. He wore a black leather jacket over a flannel shirt and faded jeans. The snow had fallen steadily while Will had been asleep, accumulating at least two inches so far, and flakes dusted the shoulders of Rex's jacket and the dark tangles of his hair.

"Fuck this fucking song," Rex grumbled, voice carrying perfectly through the crisp and quiet air. "And fuck Christmas right up its evergreen-scented ass with a candy cane."

Will snorted a quiet laugh, but cut it short when Rex looked up and directly at his window. A spark of panic sent Will's pulse racing as he leaned back in the chair and out of view.

"Record a fucking Christmas album, they said," Rex groused. "It'll be great, they said. Do some covers and a couple of original songs, what could be easier, they said."

Will's mind raced as he sat in the dark, hands clinging tight to the arms of the chair. He was listening in on Rex's creative process as he worked on a Christmas love song. Carter was never going to believe this. Hell, Will was having a hard time believing it himself. He checked the time on the clock radio across the room and was surprised to find it was shortly after midnight. Rex must have finished his set at the Side-Eye and come right back to the hotel.

Waves of gentle affection pulsed through Will at the thought. Instead of staying at the bar and drinking and being hit on by a bunch of hot guys, Rex had come back to write his song. This was a glimpse of the man underneath the image, so different from the laughing party-boy picture Will saw on Instagram and Twitter. This Rex was a serious songwriter, and Will's attraction maybe turned a little more toward desire.

Rex softly played the guitar, humming to himself. It wasn't a song Will was familiar with, and he could absolutely identify each of Rex's songs by hearing just a few chords. From what Will could tell, Rex had the melody of the song but was having trouble with the lyrics. Will hummed quietly along with Rex, his head trying to make sense of what his heart was feeling.

"Something something Christmastime," Rex sang, and even the goddamn nonsense lyrics sounded amazing.

The music stopped, and the resulting silence sounded lonely. Will eased up to the edge of the chair to be able to see the patio. Rex slouched in the metal chair, legs stretched out, head tipped back, and eyes closed. He hugged the guitar to him like a child with his favorite stuffed animal. Snow swirled around him, some landing on and sliding off the instrument's polished wood.

After some time watching Rex sitting there unmoving, Will started to feel like a creeper. He needed to get some sleep if he was going to be worth anything at work the next day. Or, rather, later that day.

Sending a silent wish down to Rex for inspiration, Will returned to his bed and climbed under the covers. He quietly hummed the melody Rex had been strumming, his nearly sleeping mind putting words to it even as sleep circled him. He mumbled them and thought briefly he should get up and write them down, but his tired mind had other ideas, and sleep swallowed him.

Chapter Three

Will didn't see Rex at breakfast the next morning, which was probably for the best considering how he'd reacted the day before. He prepared a plate—blushing and smiling when he dropped the hash browns on top of his scrambled eggs—then sat at a small table near the doorway. As he ate, he looked through Rex's social media accounts. Pictures of him playing at the Side-Eye on Instagram and Facebook, along with posts encouraging people to attend his shows. Will suspected Rex had a personal assistant, maybe that man he had shouted at the other night.

But on Twitter, Will came across a single tweet that he knew had come from Rex himself. *Tough to get the lyrics down sometimes, but a quiet night in the snow is always nice.*

A shiver of delight went through Will when he read the tweet. He had been part of Rex's quiet moment, whether or not Rex himself knew it. Smiling, Will resumed eating and quietly hummed the melody Rex had been playing the night before.

> *One stocking hangs by the fireplace*
> *But I'm lonelier by far this Christmas Eve*

SNOWFLAKES AND SONG LYRICS

The words bubbled to the top of his mind, a perfect match to the melody. Will sat back in the chair and stared at the wall. His heart pounded, and a fine layer of sweat covered his body.

He had words that went with Rex's music. He could share the words with Rex and help him write his song. They could work on the lyrics together, come up with the perfect Christmas song while stranded at this slightly shabby motel. Rex could get the chance to know Will and understand that he had just been flabbergasted at meeting Rex, which was why he'd acted so stupid. And Rex would like that Will was someone who still used the word *flabbergasted*.

Reality barged in on his daydream and stomped all over it.

Not only was Rex a complete stranger, but he was also a singer and songwriter. He wouldn't want anyone to help him write his song. That kind of help would mean Will would get a songwriting credit and kick off a host of legal ramifications that Will could not possibly understand.

Also, Will was a clumsy bear of a man, and Rex was the exact opposite.

So, fine. There it was. He could listen to Rex work on his song as much as he wanted, but he needed to stay out of it. There was no reason he should even consider helping Rex with the lyrics to his Christmas song. No. Absolutely not.

With that decided, Will resumed eating, working hard not to notice his mind toying with the lyrics in the background.

❄

THAT EVENING, WILL WAS ALREADY SITTING AT THE window when Rex opened the sliding door and stepped out onto the patio. Will had turned off all the lights in his room and left the sheer curtain open a couple of inches so he could peek around the edge. He watched Rex tune the guitar, trying not to think about how it would feel for Rex's fingers to touch him.

When he was satisfied with his tuning, Rex strummed the now-familiar melody and softly sang,

> *Christmastime is here again*
> *And here I go missing you again*

The singing and strumming stopped, and even from three floors up, Will heard his exasperated sigh.

"I'm just not in that place right now," Rex muttered.

He started playing again, but this time a very familiar tune that Will knew the words to. It was Rex's song, "Lights Out, No One's Home," and it was one of Will's personal favorites. He moved even closer to the window screen, breath fogging in the cold air as he stared down into the courtyard. This was like his own personal Rex Garland concert, and he couldn't wait to tell Carter about it. When Rex finished that song, he went right into "Clean Slate," another upbeat number, and Will quietly sang along.

When he finished that song, Rex sat with the guitar in his lap and looked up into the clear night sky. Will followed Rex's gaze, taking in the cold, silent stars spread out above them.

"I wish I may, I wish I might, have the wish I wish tonight," Rex said. "I wish for the lyrics to a great Christmas song. Period, the end."

The sliding door behind Rex opened, and a man leaned out.

"Jesus Christ, Rex, it's freezing out here," the man said. "You need to save your voice."

"I thought I needed to write a goddamn Christmas song, Earl," Rex snapped back.

"You do, but not out in the cold. Get in here!"

Rex grumbled as he got up and disappeared through the sliding door, shutting it firmly behind him.

Will pulled the sheer curtain over the window and crossed to the bed. He slid beneath the covers, shivering delightedly at the soft chill against his bare skin, and lay with his eyes closed as he thought about Rex. For someone as popular as he was, Rex seemed lonely. The refrain from the Christmas song ran on a loop in his brain, and he couldn't help adding his words to it.

One stocking hangs by the fireplace
But I'm lonelier by far this Christmas Eve

He was pretty happy with those lyrics, and he thought Rex might be as well. Will wouldn't want any credit for the lyrics. Just knowing Rex sang words Will had come up with would be all the reward he'd need. But what could he do with them? He couldn't message him on Facebook or tweet them to him because Rex would know who he was. And even if he created an account just for that purpose, there were ways to find IP addresses and locations. No, Will would need to get the lyrics to Rex in a way that couldn't be traced back to him. Like in the days before the internet when people used to send secret admirer letters.

Will sat up in bed and looked toward the window, his heart beating fast. Secret admirer letters... or maybe an anonymous note left someplace Rex was sure to find it. Someplace he visited every night. Will's stomach cramped from the excitement of his idea. How could he pull it off?

Sleep wouldn't come for him now, so he got up and pulled on boxer briefs and a T-shirt. He switched on the desk lamp and moved aside the sheer curtain to look down to the courtyard. It was empty, and a thrill went through him as he considered what he was planning. Could he really do this?

A search of the desk drawer produced stationery and envelopes with the hotel's name and address printed on them. Will decided that since he would be leaving the note in the hotel courtyard, it would be okay to use the printed stationery. He got a hotel-branded pen out of the drawer and closed his eyes as he thought about the lyrics. He only wanted to give Rex a creative nudge, not write the song for him.

He had crumpled up five sheets of paper before he was satisfied with his penmanship and the wording:

Rex,

I really like the music you've got for your Christmas song. I know you're having trouble coming up with lyrics, so how about a nudge? Feel free to use this at no charge: "One stocking hangs by the fireplace, but I'm lonelier by far this Christmas Eve."

He signed it, *A Longtime Fan.*

Will set the envelope aside and dressed in black sweats and a black pullover and grabbed his black hoodie out of the closet. He slipped the envelope and his room keycard in separate pockets of his sweatpants before checking the courtyard once more. It was still empty, so Will stepped out of his room, leaving the desk lamp on. His heart beat fast as he walked quickly down the hall.

He couldn't believe he was about to do this. His brain seemed to be arguing both for and against the idea, but his heart urged him onward.

Forgoing the elevator, Will took the stairs to the first floor, where he slipped unnoticed through the lobby and down the adjacent hallway. It was quiet along the hall, just some muted sounds of late night talk shows making their way through the heavy room doors. Will kept his eyes fixed on the red EXIT sign at the end of the hall, hoping no one stepped out of their room.

He reached the far corner of the hallway where the EXIT sign buzzed overhead. A door on one side of the hall led to the parking lot, while another door opposite opened onto the courtyard. Will cupped his hands to either side of his face and peered through the glass into the courtyard. It was empty, and he carefully pushed the door open and stepped outside.

A cold wind stung his cheeks and tousled his hair. He shivered and pulled his hood up, then made sure he could get back inside before letting the door click shut behind him. Will glanced up at the lamp in his window, glad to see the sheer curtain really did block a lot of details. Using his room window as a guide, Will walked quickly through the courtyard until he reached the patio outside Rex's room. The windows were dark, and Will took a cautious step onto the patio and set the envelope on the table.

The wind immediately snatched the envelope off the table and tossed it to the concrete.

"Dammit," Will whispered, squatting to pick up the envelope.

He dug into the snow at the edge of the patio and found a stone the size of his palm in a tiny, barren flowerbed and used that to weigh the envelope down. Satisfied with it, he looked up at his own window once more, then hurried to the door and ducked back inside the hotel.

Thoughts fluttered through his brain, not one of them stopping long enough for him to be able to focus on it. His heart pounded, and his face felt flushed.

There was no going back now.

Chapter Four

After very little sleep, Will got up the next morning and looked out the window. The stone he'd used to keep his note in place had been moved to a far edge of the table, and the envelope was gone. A flutter of excitement went through him, and Will hurried through his morning routine and out the door to breakfast.

Rex sat at one of the tables with Earl, the man Will had seen him talking with a couple of times. There were no other guests in the breakfast nook at that time, so Will listened to their conversation as he fixed himself a plate.

"I'm telling you, Earl, if you're the one who put these fucking lyrics out there, I'll kill you," Rex said.

Something inside Will clenched tight at the anger in Rex's tone. Oh shit. Had Rex misunderstood Will's gesture?

"I didn't do it," Earl said. "I swear, Rex. That note did not come from me."

"You didn't have somebody else leave it?"

"Nope. That came from someone neither of us knows."

"Well, shit." Rex sounded put out, and Will risked a glance at their table, seeing Rex slouched in his chair and staring at the note lying open before him.

"They're good lyrics," Earl said.

Will blushed a bit before turning away to hide his smile.

"I know they're good lyrics," Rex said. "But who are they from?"

"You've got a secret admirer here in the hotel, apparently," Earl said. "Come on, eat up. We've gotta get to that photo shoot."

"Yeah, all right."

Will had been listening to Rex and Earl and not paying attention to what he was doing. Because of this, he'd piled way too much food on his plate. He carried it and a cup of coffee to a table on the other side of the breakfast nook from Rex and Earl and sat down.

"I do like them," Rex said, then quietly sang the lyrics.

> *One stocking hangs by the fireplace*
> *But I'm lonelier by far this Christmas Eve*

Will thought he might pass out.

"See? Now you've got someplace to start," Earl said. "Come on. We need to leave."

Will watched them drop their trays off and walk out into the lobby. When they were gone, he let out a breath and laughed as a rush of joy surged through him. Rex Garland liked his lyrics. Rex Garland had sung something Will had written!

This was crazy and exciting, but mostly crazy.

❄

"You didn't!" Carter shouted.

He once again wore a headband, this one bright red, and his

hair puffed up over it like a mushroom cap. His eyes widened to a comical size, and spots of pink burned in his cheeks.

"I did!" Will said with a laugh. "Can you believe it?"

Carter blinked rapidly and looked away as he put a hand over his mouth.

"Wait, are you crying?" Will asked.

Carter continued to look away as he waved at the phone. "I'm fine."

"What's going on?" Will said, lowering his voice. He was propped up by pillows in the bed and brought the phone closer. "Are you okay?"

"I'm so proud," Carter said and finally looked back at the phone with a big, bright smile. "All the lessons I've taught you over the years have not been wasted."

Will rolled his eyes. "All right now."

"I was so afraid you'd end up sad and alone, your anus closed up so, so tight." Carter held up a tightly clenched fist in demonstration, making a face of extreme exertion.

A laugh exploded out of Will despite the fact that he knew better than to encourage him. Carter laughed along with him, and when Will finally got himself under control, he glared gently at the phone's camera.

"That was uncalled for."

Carter closed his eyes and nodded. "Thank you."

"That wasn't a compliment."

"Maybe not to you." Carter smiled.

"And my anus will never be able to close that tight again after I slept with that cop you introduced me to."

Carter widened his eyes. "Oh my God, same!" He thought a moment. "I wonder if he's on Grindr."

"You're going to need a bigger bottle of lube," Will said.

"You've got that right." Carter turned away from the phone and shouted, "Alexa! Reorder lube."

SNOWFLAKES AND SONG LYRICS

Will laughed and shook his head. "You're a mess."

Carter gently touched the tips of his poofed-up hair. "Who? Me?"

"Yes, you. And I love you for it."

"I love you right back, *mon ami*." Carter brought the phone closer to his face. "Now tell me all about it once more."

Will explained it all again as Carter listened with rapt attention.

"Astounding," Carter whispered once Will had finished.

"It's really not that big of a deal—"

"What?" Carter shrieked. "It is absolutely a big deal! You took it upon yourself to sneak song lyrics to Rex Garland. *The* Rex Garland, whom you have already talked with at the breakfast buffet. This is a major gigantic massive huge deal! I'm aghast. I'm totally aghast." Carter shook his head and wiped away an imaginary tear. "It's unusual for you to do something like this. I'm so proud of you. How do you feel about it?"

"Completely freaked," Will said. "I mean, what the hell was I thinking? I'm no songwriter."

"Sing it for me."

"What? No!"

"Come on!" Carter whined. "You've been singing it to him in your fantasies for days now. Sing it to me just once."

Will blushed and looked away from the phone. "I don't sing well."

Carter made an annoying buzzer sound. "Wrong! I've heard you do karaoke. You crushed 'Livin' on a Prayer' at Tuneless Mary's."

"You were drunk."

"So were you," Carter said, then affected a privileged air and said in his best Bette Davis impression, "I know talent when I hear it, William, and you, sir, have it in spades!"

"Fine, I'll do it," Will said, "just so you'll stop massacring Bette Davis impersonators worldwide."

"I shall take afront to that comment at a later time since I'm currently all aflutter for your performance."

Will cleared his throat, took a breath, shifted his gaze away from the phone, and sang the words he'd only been humming up to that point.

One stocking hangs by the fireplace
But I'm lonelier by far this Christmas Eve

Carter was silent, and when Will worked up the nerve to look back at the phone, he found him smiling with a hand against his cheek.

"It's beautiful," Carter said.

"Stop it."

"I mean it."

Will lifted his eyebrows. "You do?"

Carter nodded. "I really do. I love the lyrics. Oh my God, in my head, I can totally hear Rex singing them."

Will sat up on the bed. "Right? Aren't they, like, the perfect Rex Garland lyrics?"

"They really are. You, my friend, are on fire!"

They laughed together. Then Carter asked, "What made you do it?"

Will blushed and shrugged. "I have no idea. I sat here and listened to him play that tune, and when I tried to go to sleep, the words just came to me. I really debated whether or not I should give him the lyrics. I mean, I thought about all the legalities of it and the royalties and all of that—"

"Of course you did," Carter said through a chuckle. "But the important thing is you did it. You took the risk, and that is a huge step for you. Now, what's your plan?"

Will frowned. "My plan?"

"You've made an anonymous introduction and gotten his attention," Carter explained. "You need to plan your next move very carefully. You don't just want to walk up and introduce yourself and tell him you're his mysterious lyricist because that would be crazy."

"Right. So crazy," Will said, nervousness curling into his stomach. What was he going to do now? He hadn't really thought about an endgame for all of this—he'd just followed his impulsive heart.

"So have you given it any thought?" Carter asked.

Will shook his head and pressed his lips together before saying, "Nope. I just sort of went for it."

"Okay, that's not a bad thing," Carter said. "But you should try to come up with some kind of plan. I mean, since you took the chance and made this first step, you should be ready for something to come next, right?"

"Right. Yep."

Carter looked at him a moment. "You a little bit freaked out now?"

Will gave a single nod. "Yep."

"Want to talk about this later?"

Will nodded again. "Yep."

Carter smiled and rested his head on his palm. "You going to be okay, Big Willie?"

A deep breath helped, somewhat, and Will nodded. "I will be. I just plunged right in without thinking this through. I'm not used to doing stuff off the cuff like this. Feels kind of disorienting."

"Well, if it helps at all, I'm really proud of you," Carter said.

"Thanks."

"All that time I've spent pestering you to approach men at the bar, or on the street, or in the park has finally paid off."

"I don't think I would have been able to do if you hadn't been encouraging me all this time."

"Oh how you talk," Carter said and waved a hand as if to brush off the compliment, but Will could see he was pleased by it. "Okay, I need to finish up my beauty regimen and hit that Grindr app."

"You be careful."

"Always. You keep me posted on how things are going out there in Utah."

"I'm in upstate New York," Will said with a grin.

"Details," Carter said. Then he looked right into the camera and added, "You take care of yourself, Will. You're the best friend I've got."

"Oh, Carter, really?" Will smiled as a warm feeling rushed through him. "I feel the same way. I couldn't wait to tell you about this craziness I've gone and gotten myself into. Thanks for listening."

"Anytime, *mon ami*," Carter said. "Now leave me to my facial while I prep for another facial later."

Will laughed and disconnected the call. He stayed in place, propped up on pillows in his bed, the phone on his chest and a warm feeling still glowing in his chest from his talk with Carter. He thought about the fun they'd had, both during the time they dated and afterwards as they became friends. With a smile on his face, Will drifted off to sleep.

❄

WILL SNORTED IN HIS SLEEP AND JERKED AWAKE. He blinked and squinted in the glare of the bedside lamp and reached out to switch it off. The only illumination came from the courtyard lamps diffused by the sheers. A breeze from the open window billowed the curtains a bit, and Will snuggled deeper beneath the covers and closed his eyes.

The quiet strum of a guitar floated through the window, and Will's eyes popped open. He sat straight up in bed and looked toward the window.

Rex was outside.

With careful movements, Will got out of bed. He shivered in the chill and grabbed his hoodie as he crept across the room. At the window, he shifted the curtains a bit and looked down into the courtyard. Rex sat at his patio table, strumming his guitar and humming. A gentle snowfall was illuminated in the light of the courtyard lamps, and Will couldn't think of a more romantic and seasonal scene. Rex's voice sounded clear and pure in the still, snowy air, and it seemed to wrap around Will's heart as he sang.

> *One stocking hangs by the fireplace*
> *But I'm lonelier by far this Christmas Eve*

Before Will could even process the fact that Rex had just sung the words Will had written, Rex continued with brand-new lyrics.

> *You're so far away, so far from my reach*
> *My heart aches for you, but my mind still*
>   *believes*
> *You'll come back to me*
> *You'll come stay with me*

Will let out a breath he hadn't realized he'd been holding. It fogged the air before him and drifted out the window. His smile was so wide it almost hurt.

Rex Garland had used his lyrics as a starting point for a Christmas song.

Will had no idea what to do, so he stood and watched Rex

play the guitar and sing through the lyrics several more times, his smile growing bigger each time.

The patio door behind Rex slid open, and the man Will had seen him with at breakfast stepped outside. His name was Earl, if Will remembered correctly, and it seemed as if he was Rex's manager.

"How's the song?" Earl asked.

"Not bad," Rex said. "Want to hear what I have?"

Earl crossed his arms tight. "Does it have to be out here? It's freezing."

Rex looked up, almost directly at Will's window, and he took a step back to make sure he wasn't seen.

"This is the perfect setting for this song," Rex said. "It's like it's Christmas Eve right here and now."

"Great," Earl grumbled. "Tell Santa I want your next Christmas residency to be someplace warm with a beach."

Rex chuckled as he played the guitar. "Where's your holiday spirit?"

"Someplace warm with a beach," Earl said. "But I'm glad to see your mood has improved the last couple of days."

"I guess my songwriting Christmas elf might have something to do with that," Rex said, then looked up at Earl. "And you swear it wasn't you?"

Earl briefly held up a hand and said, "I swear," before crossing his arms tight once again.

Rex played what he had of the song, and Will's heart felt as if it danced along with the tempo.

"It's good," Earl said. "I like it. Can we go inside now?"

Rex continued to play and seemed to be talking mostly to himself as he said, "I need to figure out the chorus, but I like what I've got so far." He looked up at Earl. "What comes to mind when you think of Christmas?"

"Being someplace warm, with a beach," Earl said.

"Dammit, Earl, this is serious," Rex said. "Come on, you got me signed up for this Christmas album. Help me out. What makes you think of Christmas?"

"Ugh, let's see." Earl looked up into the snowfall. "Stockings, Christmas tree, presents, holiday lights, snow, cookies, mistletoe, family." He turned for the patio door. "Can we go inside now? Come on, this cold air is doing nothing for your voice, and you've still got two weeks of shows."

"Fine, all right."

Rex got up and pushed in the chair as Earl fled into the hotel room. Before Rex followed Earl inside, he picked up the stone Will had used to weigh down his envelope and held it in his hand. Looking around the courtyard, Rex said quietly, "Thanks for the assist, Christmas elf."

He set the stone in the center of the small table and went into his room, sliding the door shut behind him.

Will stood at the window and stared down at Rex's patio for a long time. His heart pounded, and he couldn't stop smiling as he watched the snow quietly accumulate on the stone and table. He finally turned away and walked to the bed where he jumped up and landed facedown. Pressing his face into a pillow, he shouted with glee before rolling onto his back and staring at the ceiling as he tried to calm his racing mind and heart.

What the hell was going on? Had he actually provided Rex Garland a songwriting nudge?

The song ran on a loop in his mind as he looked at the bedside clock and grimaced. It was going to be a long day tomorrow if he didn't get to sleep soon.

He peeled off the hoodie and slid under the covers, closing his eyes and taking deep breaths to try and get himself into a tranquil state. Eventually, he slipped into sleep, the sound of Rex's voice echoing in the back of his mind.

Chapter Five

"You go out drinking last night?"

Will looked up from his breakfast to find Doreen, the hotel housekeeper assigned to his room, looking him over.

"No, just couldn't get to sleep," Will said and smiled as he sipped his coffee.

"Oh?" Doreen took a few steps closer and lowered her voice. "Didya get lucky?"

"Nope." Will grinned. "Just couldn't shut my mind off."

Doreen nodded. "I get that too sometimes. Too many thoughts to process before the system shuts down."

"Right," Will said. "You sound like you have an IT background."

"My daughter does," Doreen said with a shrug. "She's been helping me with my computer. You done up in your room?"

"Yeah, I'm heading out after I finish this cup of coffee. Oh, leave the window open a bit when you're through, please."

"You one of those fresh air addicts?" Doreen asked, giving him a suspicious look.

"Well, fresh air is nice," Will said. "But the heating unit is working a bit too well, and the room gets way too warm."

"Didya have maintenance take a look?"

"I did, yeah, but he wasn't able to do much with it."

"Who was up there?" Doreen asked.

"Not sure. He was tall and bald."

"That was Steve. He's kind of lazy. I'll give Sarge a note about it." Doreen jotted something on her clipboard, then gave him a nod. "You have a good day now. Try some valerian root tea before bed. Smells like stinky feet, but it helps calm your mind."

"Okay, thanks," Will said with a chuckle. "I'll make a note of that."

After Doreen walked off, Will looked around the breakfast area. No sign of Rex or Earl, just a couple of parents with kids, some intense business types sitting on their own, and an older couple looking through tourist pamphlets.

Will chugged the remainder of his coffee, delivered his tray to the drop-off section, and filled his stainless steel insulated cup with coffee from a fresh pot. Outside, a blast of frigid air made him curse and bunch down into his jacket. He could smell snow in the air and glanced into the wind toward the west. A thick bank of gray snow clouds crept toward the region. Looked like they were about to get dumped on.

❄

WILL STRUGGLED TO FOCUS DURING HIS WORKDAY. IF HE wasn't looking out the window watching the snow fall harder each passing minute, he was quietly humming Rex's Christmas song and doodling pictures of a guitar and a variety of Christmas-related objects like a decorated tree, wrapped presents, and a whole army of candy canes.

"You a big Christmas fan?"

Will looked up to find Andrew Kuspa, a member of the team he'd been assisting, standing next to his lunch table and looking down at his sketches. Andrew gave off a somewhat sneaky and snarky vibe, which put Will's defenses up. He sat back and shrugged, hoping it came across as casual as he shifted his hands to cover the doodles and lyrics he'd been writing down, then crossing off.

"I don't know if I'd call myself a big Christmas fan, but it is one of my favorite holidays."

Andrew nodded as he stretched a kink out of his neck. He was slender and wiry, his blond hair expensively styled and the perfect amount of matching stubble nicely trimmed around his square jaw. Blue eyes completed his all-American look, and Will tried not to envy him too much.

"I get it. All your shopping done yet?" Andrew pulled out the chair next to Will and sat.

"Oh, um, yeah. I got it all done before I left to come here. Online shopping mostly."

"You a fan of Black Friday?"

Will shook his head. "Not really. Too crazy for me."

"Crowds make you nervous?"

"Oh, um, I don't know—"

Will was cut off by the arrival of Bridget Caruso, their team manager. She was as well put together as Andrew, with light brown hair that framed her heart-shaped face and almost perfectly matched the color of her eyes. Will sometimes wondered if Bridget dyed her hair that specific color just to make them match.

"There's talk of closing the office early," Bridget said.

"Oh really?" Will looked out the window at the steady snowfall. "Probably a good idea."

"I had plans tonight," Andrew said with a pout, then waved a hand toward the window. "But I bet my friends chicken out because of all this."

"'All this' meaning a snowstorm that's been predicted all week?" Bridget said.

Andrew rolled his eyes. "Who has time for the news?"

Will and Bridget exchanged a look and said at the same time, "I do."

"You're both nerds."

Bridget tapped the fitness bracelet on her wrist. "It's almost time for the meeting."

"Come on, Will, gather up your elf practice drawings, and let's go," Andrew said before he stood up. "Will loves Christmas and likes to doodle things related to the season."

Bridget looked at him with perfectly threaded eyebrows raised.

"I was just thinking of the holidays coming up and was doodling, that's all," Will said, shooting Andrew a dirty look that was missed because the man was looking out at the snow.

"It is a fun holiday," Bridget said, then sighed. "If you can find the right toys for your kids. Anyway, let's get a move on."

Will closed his notebook and followed them down the hall. Rex's voice and lyrics echoed in the back of his mind, and he couldn't help a small smile.

During the meeting, Will had his notebook open to a clean page, ready to jot down anything important. He was a few seats away from Andrew and Bridget both, and even though he tried to focus on work, his mind kept delivering possible lyrics. Earlier he'd written in his notebook the lyrics Rex had so far, and he flipped back to that page to read them again.

> One stocking hangs by the fireplace
> But I'm lonelier by far this Christmas Eve
> You're so far away, so far from reach
> My heart aches for you, but my mind still
>   believes

You'll come back to me
You'll come stay with me
Weatherman says we're bound to get snow
But my heart's not feeling that holiday
   glow
Without you by my side
This Christmastime

He smiled even as his heart ached for some kind of face-to-face connection with Rex. The secret lyrics were fun, but Will wanted to get to know Rex more than as a fan. He just didn't know how would Rex handle finding out Will was his secret elf supplying him lyrics. Will thought about Rex asking Earl what came to mind when he thought Christmas, and a couple of lines came to him which he quickly jotted down.

Can I pretend you're mine for Christmas?
Can I wish for you this Christmas Eve?
The two of us could be Christmas-cookie
   delicious
Can I pretend you're mine for Christmas?

He sat back in his chair and read the lines several times. His heart pounded, and his face felt warm. Had he just come up with the chorus of the song?

"All right, so it's official," Bridget said as she pushed her chair back and stood up.

Will blinked and looked up, watching as everyone else stood as well. What had he missed?

"Everyone be careful driving home and call the office main phone number tomorrow morning to see if we're going to be open tomorrow. This snow's supposed to go into the weekend."

Chapter Six

The drive to the Williamsville Inn took three times as long as usual. Even though it was midafternoon, Will figured every other business had decided to send workers home early because the roads were jammed with cars slipping and sliding through snow and slush. He kept running the new words he'd written down through his head and decided the Christmas cookie line needed to be changed. By the time he reached the hotel parking lot, his fingers ached from gripping the steering wheel, and it was already getting dark.

Doreen had left his window open a couple of inches, and the room was at a comfortable temperature when he walked in. He sighed with relief, then checked the time on his phone, surprised to find it was almost five o'clock. So much for a surprise half day. Quickly changing out of work clothes into jeans and a sweatshirt, he laced up his waterproof hiking boots, grabbed his coat and notebook, and then headed out again. If the drive back to the hotel was any indication, a lot of people were out of work, and Will wanted to get food before the rush of diners.

He left his car in the lot and trudged toward the rib joint he'd eaten at before, which was only three blocks away. With the hood up and his head down, he forged a path through the accumulated snow as he headed into the wind, telling himself the walk back would be easier with it at his back. Tears streamed down his cheeks, and his lips felt dry and cracked.

At the restaurant, he stood just inside the door and made faces as he worked on getting the blood flowing to his face again. There were two empty tables waiting, and the hostess led him to the smaller table in the corner. He exchanged pleasantries with the young waiter, talking mostly about the snow before Will ordered a double portion of ribs with a side of macaroni and cheese and a Guinness. He wouldn't be able to eat all of the ribs, but he wanted to have some extra to take back to his room and store in the mini refrigerator.

The final open table was taken by a snow-dusted couple, and Will opened his notebook, turning his attention to the lyrics he'd written during the work meeting.

> *Can I pretend you're mine for Christmas?*
> *Can I wish for you this Christmas Eve?*
> *The two of us could be Christmas-cookie*
>   *delicious*
> *Can I pretend you're mine for Christmas?*

Yeah, that Christmas cookie line needed to go. He chewed the end of his pen and stared at the hostess stand, where the young girl twirled the end of her hair around her finger as she scrolled through an app on her phone. She pursed her lips and blew a bubble with her gum, and Will smiled before he wrote the new line.

> *All I want from Santa is your kisses*

SNOWFLAKES AND SONG LYRICS

Will sat back and smiled. Yeah, that was a lot better.

The waiter brought his food, the plate piled high with ribs and the macaroni and cheese a golden yellow mound of creamy delight in a separate dish. Will's smiled widened as he picked up his fork at the same time the restaurant door opened. A man came in amid a swirl of snow, his dark hair and matching beard dusted with it. The new arrival stomped snow off his boots, ran a hand through his hair, and smiled at the hostess.

Will's heart jumped when he realized it was Rex.

He quickly closed his notebook and placed it on the seat beside him. Rex asked the hostess where he could pick up a takeout order, his deep, smooth voice seeming to wrap around Will's pounding heart. The girl pointed in Will's direction, and his heartbeat doubled when Rex looked right at him.

And smiled.

Will smiled back, feeling ridiculous and somehow guilty for being caught sitting behind a massive plate of ribs. Jesus, could he look any more like an overeater?

Rex walked toward him, gaze locked on Will and that smile crooking up one corner of his beautiful mouth.

"Hey there," Rex said as he stopped beside Will's table. "Hashies on your omelet, right? The budget farmer's omelet at the Williamsville Inn?"

Will's blush deepened so much he feared flames might burst into life on his cheeks. "Yeah. That's me." A tiny, stubborn logic center in his brain that managed to stay engaged kicked into gear, while the rest of his mind ran around waving its arms and screaming, "Rex Garland is talking to us!" The logic center pushed some words into his mouth and got his arm moving, so he stuck out a hand.

"My name's Will. Will Johnson."

Rex grinned and clasped Will's hand tight. "Are you a spy? Like Bond, James Bond?"

A loud, horrible-sounding laugh slipped past the one functioning logic center. Will quickly closed his mouth and shook his head. "Nope. Just an ordinary guy."

"You kidding?" Rex said with a tilt of his head. "You're the guy that started the budget farmer's omelet trend. You're far from ordinary, Will Will Johnson. And I'm Rex Garland."

Rex released his hand, and it dropped into Will's lap. For a terrifying moment, Will was afraid his hand would shift to cup himself, putting Rex's touch right against his crotch. But apparently, he had a bit more presence of mind left than he'd feared because his hand remained still. Before he could tell Rex he knew damn well who he was and loved all his music, Rex spoke again.

"That's a lot of meat." Rex nodded down toward Will's plate.

"Oh, I got a double portion," Will said. "I want to have some to take back to my room and put in the refrigerator. My office will probably be closed tomorrow because of the storm, and I wanted to have something there to eat so I didn't have to go out again. Not that I mind going outside. It's just, with the snow and everything, I'd rather just stay in the room. Most likely go down to breakfast, but, you know, that's still in the hotel and not outside."

Will managed to stop talking by pressing his lips together tight. He made a face up at Rex and said, "Sorry. I babble sometimes."

Rex's half-smile hadn't slipped a bit. In fact, it bloomed into a full smile.

"I'm the same way." He gestured toward the pickup window a few feet away from Will's table. "I've got a takeout order waiting that's nearly identical to yours. Great minds, Will Will Johnson. You be careful not to get lost out there in the snow."

"Yeah, okay. You too."

Rex walked away, and Will looked over his shoulder to watch as he approached the carryout counter set in the corner behind where Will sat. Damn, Rex had an amazing ass. How many squats did he do every day?

Will turned back to his meal. He tried to tune out Rex's voice behind him as he paid for his meal, but the deep timbre was impossible to ignore. Will picked at his ribs and ate small portions of his mac and cheese, afraid to take larger bites in case Rex spoke to him on his way out the door.

As if picking up on Will's anxiety, Rex did just that a few minutes later.

"Bundle up when you leave. The temperature's dropping fast," Rex said.

Will nodded fast. "I will. Thanks. You be careful with your meat."

Heat flamed across his face, and he tore his gaze from Rex's as he mentally cursed himself. What the hell was wrong with him? To Will's combined horror and excitement, Rex leaned down and lowered his voice as he whispered, "I always treat my meat real nice. I think every guy should, don't you?"

Will managed to meet Rex's gaze for a moment and, still blushing furiously, nodded again. "Yes."

Rex winked, lifted two large bags stacked with carryout containers, and said, "Gotta get back before my manager sends out a search party. See you at breakfast."

Will watched him walk away, then put his head in his hands and stared down at his plate. What the hell was wrong with him?

Nerves had dampened his appetite, so Will had quite a bit of food to take back to his room. By the time he'd trudged through the snow and entered the hotel lobby with the heavy bag in one hand, his fingers were numb from the cold. He managed to fit all the food in the mini fridge and then stripped out of his clothes, damp from the snow, and stretched out on his bed to watch some TV. The window was open a couple of inches, and the curtains puffed in and out with the wind gusts. Will thought it looked like a ghost taking deep, meditative breaths and, smiling at the image, drifted off to sleep.

❄

WILL WOKE UP A COUPLE HOURS LATER FEELING COLD AND needing to pee. After using the bathroom, he pulled on sweats and his hoodie and stepped to the window. More snow had accumulated while he'd been napping. A lot more snow. Because the courtyard was surrounded by three stories of rooms on three sides and the single-story hallway on the fourth, there was very little drifting due to wind. Snow still fell through the glow of the lamps and glittered where it had fallen. It was beautiful, and Will sat in the desk chair and watched for a long time, his gaze often moving back to the table where Rex usually sat. There was at least a foot of snow piled on top, and Will smiled as he thought about sitting at that table across from Rex and helping him push the snow aside.

Then he had another even better idea, and he got out more stationery and opened his notebook to where he'd written the lyrics for the chorus. He thought a moment, then wrote a quick note:

Rex,

Loving the progress you're making on the song. I thought maybe you might be able to use these lyrics for the chorus. Enjoy the snow!

> *Can I pretend you're mine for Christmas?*
> *Can I wish for you this Christmas Eve?*
> *All I want from Santa is your kisses*
> *Can I pretend you're mine for Christmas?*

He read the note over a few times before signing it, *Your Long-*

time Fan. Then he folded it and slid it into an envelope, on which he wrote *Rex.*

With that done, Will pulled on his socks and boots, then grabbed his coat, the room keycard, and the envelope and set off down the hall. The lobby was empty once again, and as he passed through, he nodded to the young guy behind the front desk. It was still pretty early, so most guests were up and watching TV, based on the muted sounds he could hear as he walked along the first-floor hallway. When he reached the door to the courtyard, he stopped to look up and down the hall. No one was around, so he pushed the release bar on the door, but it remained in place. He tried again, and the door moved a bit but still didn't open.

"What the hell?"

"Snow's blocking it."

The voice startled a shout out of Will, and he turned to find Doreen standing by the door across from him that opened to the parking lot. She wore a jacket and had a large purse slung over one shoulder. An unlit cigarette trembled between two fingers.

"Open window doesn't give you enough fresh air?" Doreen asked.

"You scared five years off my life," Will said.

She held up the cigarette. "Guess I'll see you in line to talk to St. Pete then, huh?"

"What are you doing here?" Will asked.

"Waiting for my daughter to pick me up," Doreen said. "Bad night for driving, but what can you do?"

"Oh." Will felt a trickle of cold air against the back of his calves and looked down. "I didn't think about the snow blocking the door."

"You're gonna need to push pretty hard," Doreen said. "Here, like this."

Before Will could decline her help, Doreen put her cigarette in her coat pocket, adjusted the strap of her purse across her shoulder, and then strode quickly toward him and shoved the door hard. It moved several inches, allowing snow to tumble in through the opening. Doreen smiled at him.

"There, see? Just needs some elbow grease." She peered through the narrow opening. "Lot prettier in the courtyard than it is out in the street where we gotta walk and drive in it."

"Yeah, um, I just wanted to go take a look around." Will shrugged. "It looked pretty from my window."

Doreen assessed him silently a moment until her phone buzzed and she drew it from her coat pocket. "That's my ride." She regarded him again. "Got your keycard to get back inside?"

"Yep, right here... oh."

Will had put the envelope in the same coat pocket as his keycard, and when he withdrew the keycard to show it to Doreen, the envelope tumbled out onto the floor. It landed front side up so that Rex's name was clearly visible.

"Oops, that's just something I forgot to throw out," Will said and crouched down quickly to retrieve it.

"Don't stay out there too long now," Doreen said as she turned away to head for the exit door. "This cold sneaks up on you."

"Yep, okay. Thanks for the help."

Will watched her light her cigarette before she opened the door and, amid a swirl of snow and smoke, vanished outside. He turned to the door behind him and, with a grunt of effort, pushed it open far enough for him to squeeze through. Protected from the wind, the snow in the courtyard was smooth and pristine, the air completely still. Will stood and simply looked around for a time, savoring the silence and beauty.

A truck rumbled down the road past the hotel, snapping Will out of his serenity. There was work to do, and he didn't want to get caught. He hated to muss up the beautiful snow, but he didn't really have a choice. Moving carefully, Will made his way to Rex's patio table and set to work.

SNOWFLAKES AND SONG LYRICS

❄

ONCE HE'D FINISHED HIS TASK, WILL STEPPED BACK AND assessed his handiwork. Everything looked perfect. He drew his phone from his pocket and checked to make sure there was still plenty of time until Rex returned. With that settled, he opened the FaceTime app and placed a call to Carter.

After a couple of rings, Carter answered the call. His face was pale and shiny with sweat, and he was propped up in bed against a number of pillows.

"Hey, Big Willie." Carter coughed a few times before giving the phone a pitiful look.

"Oh no, you're sick," Will said, his good mood lowering a bit.

"I'll be fine," Carter said and looked away dramatically. "Don't worry about me."

Will chuckled. "You must not be too sick if you can still act so dramatic."

"It's just a cold," Carter said with a heavy sigh. "I'm sure it's not the consumption."

"Poor thing," Will said with a pout. "Do you need me to send a hot doctor to make a house call?"

"No, no, don't worry about me. I'll just find one on Grindr when we hang up." Carter pushed himself higher up the pillows and coughed a few times. "What's going on there in Alaska?"

"I'm in upstate New York."

Carter squinted at the screen. "It doesn't look like it. Are you outside?"

"I am," Will said and couldn't help smiling. "I'm in the courtyard outside Rex's room."

"The courtyard?" Carter's eyes grew wide. "The place where you left him song lyrics?"

"Shhh," Will said, looking all around for any open windows. The only one he saw open was his own, and he turned his attention back to Carter. "I'm leaving him another lyric suggestion."

"What? For the love of... Do you think you're Captain and Tennille all of a sudden?"

A surprised laugh surged up from Will's core, echoing around the walls of the courtyard. He slapped a hand over his mouth and stared at the phone as Carter collapsed into a mix of laughter and deep, hacking coughs. Carter dropped the phone, and Will found himself looking at a view of the ceiling fan over the bed as Carter coughed up what sounded like a massive glob of phlegm.

When he picked the phone up again, Carter looked completely spent. Red spots glowed on his cheeks, and his forehead glistened with greasy sweat.

"I think I coughed up something out of *The X-Files*," Carter said. "My apologies you had to witness that rather disgusting scene."

"You okay?" Will asked.

Carter nodded and slowly drew in a breath. "I can actually breathe a bit better. See? All I needed to do was talk to my good friend."

"And throw down a reference to some obscure singing duo."

"They are hardly obscure."

"Anyway, do you want to see the patio and table?"

Carter nodded and looked more alert. "I do. Show me."

Will approached the patio and touched the button to switch to the camera on the back of his phone. He looked at the screen, watching Carter's expression as he slowly panned back and forth, showing Carter what he'd done.

"Is that... Is that a tiny snowman?" Carter asked, squinting at the phone. "The lighting is weird there."

"Yeah, they have these old-time lampposts out here. See?" Will slowly turned to show Carter the trident-style lampposts with frosted glass shades covering the bulbs. Snow fell through the yellow lamplight, and Will couldn't help smiling. "Oh, and that window on the top floor with the light on? That's my room."

"You know this is like some goddamn Julia Roberts or Reese Witherspoon movie, right?"

Will switched the app to use the camera on the front of the phone again so Carter could see his face. "I know. Only it's me and Rex Garland."

"Look at your ridiculously large smile," Carter said with a grin. "You look happier than you've been in a long time."

"It's been kind of fun," Will said. "And exciting and nerve-racking."

"And romantic as hell."

"That too."

"Show me the snowman again," Carter said.

Will changed to the other camera once more and studied his creation as well. He'd used the snow piled on top of the table to build a snowman about two feet tall. Digging into the snow beneath the window of Rex's room, he'd uncovered a gravel-lined flowerbed and pried up a few pebbles to use for the face, making sure the snowman appeared to be looking at the patio door. He found a long, thin branch beneath a Japanese maple near one of the lampposts and broke it in half. Propping the envelope against the snowman, he placed the sticks at a downward angle to make it look like the snowman was holding onto the envelope.

"You, my good friend, have graduated to hopeless romantic."

"Yeah," Will said. "I have."

"Where do you see this going?" Carter asked.

Will stared at the snowman. Where did he see this crazy stunt going? Would it end up with him at some point meeting Rex? If that happened, how would Rex react? He hadn't seemed angry about the initial suggested lyrics, but what would he think if he knew Will was the mystery lyric writer? Will wasn't really Rex's type, based on the singer's Instagram account. There was no way he could compete with all those muscular men in tiny bathing suits Rex continually posed with or the hot guys lined up in front of every stage, staring raptly up at Rex as he sang. So what was Will's ultimate goal? If he was honest with himself, his fantasy had always been for Rex to realize Will was perfect for him, even if he wasn't a perfect physical specimen. But how would that even work? Rex performed all over the country, singing to sold-out crowds of horny and handsome men and building his fanbase, while Will sat in a cubicle manipulating data in spreadsheets. Not really a perfect match.

"Big Willie? You still there?" Carter's voice was softer, gentle, as if he knew his question had struck a nerve.

After taking a breath and managing to smile, Will switched to the front camera. "Yeah, I'm here. I, um, I haven't thought that far ahead."

Carter knew him too well for that to go over, and true to his nature, he called him out on it.

"I find that hard to believe. You're a born planner. Hell, I bet you were born the exact day and time the doctor predicted."

Will nodded in agreement. His mother had always told him she could have set her watch by his birth, which, while weird, seemed to have carried through to the rest of his life.

"So what's the big picture look like inside that handsome, bearded head of yours?" Carter asked. "Where do you see this ending up?"

A light went on behind the drapes of the room next to Rex's, and adrenaline rushed through Will's system.

"Someone's here," Will whispered to the phone and began the slow, plodding journey back to the door.

"Who? Rex? Is Rex there?"

"No, someone in the room beside his. I need to get out of this courtyard. Let me call you back."

"Okay, be careful," Carter said, then disconnected.

Will knocked as much snow as possible off his boots before stepping into the hallway, then pulled the door closed, making sure it latched securely. The cold had gotten in under his coat, and he shivered as he crossed the lobby to the elevators. The inside of the elevator was all mirrors, and Will stared at himself, taking in his dark blond hair, damp from falling snow, his matching beard, and dark blue eyes. He was at least fifteen pounds overweight, probably more since he'd been less active at the hotel. What did he think was going to happen with this little game he was playing? Someone like Rex Garland would never be interested in someone like him. Had Will really been hoping that Rex was going to fall in love with him because he wrote some simple song lyrics? His self-delusion had been running really deep lately.

The elevator doors opened, and he stepped out into the hallway. It was quiet on his floor because most of the rooms up here were being remodeled, and he'd only seen a couple of other guests in the hallway since he'd arrived. Will liked the quiet, but at times like this, the quiet meant the voices in his head got louder.

Rex had spoken first in line for the breakfast buffet, he said to himself.

He called you out for putting hash browns on your eggs, that cutting voice responded, *which meant he was calling you out about your weight.*

But he stopped to talk to me at the restaurant earlier, Will tried.

The cruel reply followed quickly: *Where you sat behind a plate heaped with food. He would never want to be with someone like you. You don't measure up to him.*

Will let himself into his room. His thoughts fought in his head as he kicked off his boots and shrugged out of his coat. He paced the length of the room, quietly arguing with himself. This was ridiculous. He'd written some poems in high school and college, but he had never written a goddamn song. What made him think he could send lyrics to Rex Garland, an established singer/songwriter? Holy hell, what kind of gall did he have to leave lyrics for him like some kind of lovestruck thirteen-year-old girl passing secret admirer notes to a schoolyard crush?

Humiliation crushed the air from his lungs and wrung any lingering joy from his heart. What the hell had he been thinking? He needed to fix this before it was too late. He could go back to the courtyard and demolish that ridiculous snowman and retrieve the note.

Will stepped to the window and looked out to make sure there was no one around. His heart gave a sudden lurch, and his stomach twisted into a tight knot of dread.

Rex stood on the patio, Will's note in hand. The patio door stood open behind him, casting light across his features as he read what Will had written.

"Oh shit," Will said, maybe a bit too loudly.

Rex's head snapped up, and Will jerked back out of sight. His breath came in short pants, and his heart banged against his ribs as if trying to escape his chest. He sat on the end of the bed, hands flat against the bedspread as he took deep, slow breaths to try and calm himself. There was no going back now. Rex had found the note, like it or not. All Will could do now was keep from interfering with Rex's creative process going forward. He had to stop these childish games.

"Is it still snowing?"

That sounded like Earl, Rex's manager.

"Yeah, no sign of letting up," Rex called back.

"What's that?" Earl must have stepped up to the sliding patio door.

"More lyrics from my secret songwriter," Rex said.

The tone of Rex's voice pulled Will up from the bed and closer to the window, standing behind the blackout drapes to stay out of sight. Rex sounded happy, like he was touched by the note.

"Is that a snowman?" Earl asked.

"Yeah, it's cute, isn't it?" Rex said, the smile evident in his voice.

Will had to see him, had to see Rex's expression. He moved to the end of the blackout curtain and leaned to the side. The sheer curtains masked too much of the details for him to see Rex's face, so he moved closer to the open window. When he was able to see around the sheers, Will saw Rex sitting in one of the chairs with his phone out and pointed at the table. Rex had placed the note, unfolded, on the table in front of the snowman, and the flash on his phone strobed as he took a photo. Earl leaned in the door, watching him.

"What do you think of the lyrics?" Earl asked.

Rex nodded as he looked at the photo on his phone. "They're good, actually." He looked up, and even from that height and distance, Will plainly saw his smile. "Really good. My secret Santa songwriter gave me a chorus."

"A chorus?" Earl held out his hand. "Let me see."

"In a minute. I want to hang out here a little longer, okay?"

"Not too long," Earl said. "Full lineup of appearances this weekend."

"A strip mall is not an appearance."

"It is to the guys who come out to see you." Earl stepped back into room. "Five minutes. I'm serious."

"Yes, Mom."

"You should have been so lucky," Earl said and slid the door shut.

Rex took a few more photos of the note and snowman arrangement before putting his phone in his jacket pocket. He stood and slowly looked around the courtyard, seeming to assess each window. Will jerked back behind the blackout curtain and held his breath as he curled his hands into fists. Had Rex seen him? What would he do if he had?

To Will's amazement, Rex started singing. He wasn't using the full power of his voice, but the cold, still air brought it up to Will's window like some kind of divine message meant just for him. And, in a way, that was exactly what it was.

> *One stocking hangs by the fireplace*
> *But I'm lonelier by far this Christmas Eve*
> *You're so far away, so far from reach*
> *My heart aches for you, but my mind still*
>   *believes*
> *You'll come back to me*
> *You'll come stay with me*
> *Weatherman says we're bound to get snow*
> *But my heart's not feeling that holiday*
>   *glow*
> *Without you by my side*
> *This Christmastime*

Rex stopped, and Will heard the rustle of paper before he continued to sing.

> *Can I pretend you're mine for Christmas?*
> *Can I wish for you this Christmas Eve?*
> *All I want from Santa is your kisses*
> *Can I pretend you're mine for Christmas?*

As he listened to Rex sing their words, Will gathered the heavy blackout curtains in his fists. Not Rex's words, not Will's words, *their* words they'd come up with together. Because it hadn't been just one of them writing those lyrics; it had been both of them.

"Thanks, my secret Santa songwriter," Rex said. "Whoever you are."

The patio door slid open, allowing the sound of a TV to sully the quiet of the courtyard before it shut again.

"Holy shit," Will whispered. He stepped away from the window and fell back across the bed. "Holy shit. He liked them. Rex really liked the lyrics."

Will pushed any questions or concerns about how everything in this crazy scenario was going to play out and let himself revel in the moment.

Rex Garland had sung his lyrics.

Chapter Seven

The snow stopped just before the Friday morning rush hour, leaving the area buried under nearly two feet of fresh accumulation. Meteorologists assured everyone the worst was over for the time being as long lists of school closings crawled along the bottom of the TV screen. Will called the phone number Bridget had provided the day before and pumped his fist when he heard the recorded announcement stating the office would be closed. He couldn't remember ever before receiving a surprise three-day weekend from work due to the weather.

He propped himself up in bed, half-watching the local news coverage of the efforts to clear the roads as he relived hearing Rex singing their lyrics the night before. Would Rex ever sing that song live? Could he sing it during his extended appearances at the Side-Eye? Will grabbed his phone and navigated to Rex's Facebook page. He scrolled through the posts, smiling at the photos of Rex in concert as he searched for the schedule Rex or his social media manager had posted listing his appearances at the Side-Eye. There it was, and Rex was playing that night and the rest of next week.

With a start, Will realized the following week would be the last full week until Christmas. His time there in Williamsville was winding down fast. And even if his assignment was extended beyond Christmas Eve, Rex's appearances at the Side-Eye would be over. The snowstorm had dropped the perfect opportunity right in Will's lap. The road crews were out in force making sure the highways were clear. Will didn't have to worry about driving to the hotel from the office, finding food, and changing clothes, then driving to the bar. All he had to do was pick his outfit and drive right to the Side-Eye.

This was it. Tonight, he would go see Rex sing live for the first time. Tonight, he would discover what it felt like to receive the full Rex Garland experience.

But he had no idea what to wear. He would be in a bar filled with men who worked out steadily. Will needed to feel good about himself if he were to be in their midst. For a decision that important, he was going to need some guidance.

❄

"Tell it to me again."

On the FaceTime app, Carter's eyes gleamed with gleeful curiosity. Or maybe it was fever. Will couldn't be certain.

"I don't know if you're really up to this," Will said. "You look even more flushed now, and maybe a little manic. When did you last take your temperature?"

"2015. Come on, tell it again. But slower this time, and with more emotion."

Will shook his head. "Not until I watch you take your temperature and you show me the readout."

Carter rolled his eyes. "Okay. But it's a rectal thermometer, you perv."

Will laughed but cut it short and gave him a stern look. "Stop stalling and get to it."

"You are the biggest killjoy."

"I love you, too," Will said patiently. "Now go."

Carter made a big production of rolling off the couch. He stomped through his apartment to the bathroom, holding up his phone so Will could see his face. By Carter's expression, it looked like every step was an effort. Will could see the bathroom counter was clean and organized as Carter picked up the thermometer, and the sight reassured him. Organization was one of Carter's predominant traits, and if the bathroom looked that good, Carter still cared enough to keep it that way.

The thermometer was the type that measured temperature within the ear canal. Carter held the phone out, allowing Will to watch him press the tip into his ear and giving him a deadpan stare as they waited. Will smirked and shook his head. Even sick as a dog, Carter was still bringing the sass. When the thermometer beeped to signal it was finished, Carter removed it and looked at the readout.

"Well?" Will said.

Carter sighed and held the thermometer up so Will could see the display: 102.4.

"Uh-huh," Will said, trying not to sound like a parent but knowing he had failed.

"So I have a fever. So what?" Carter said. "It's not a surprise."

"Take something to bring that fever down," Will said. "Right now."

"Oh my God, you don't understand me at all!" Carter whined like a petulant child.

But he propped the phone on the bathroom counter so Will could watch as he swallowed a couple of ibuprofen. Carter turned to the phone, opening his mouth and sticking out his tongue to prove he'd swallowed the pills.

"Very good," Will said in his best patronizing tone. "Now get into bed and under the covers. Are you drinking fluids?"

"I went to the water sports room in the local bathhouse last night—does that count?"

Will made a face. "Not sure that's the same thing."

Carter shrugged as he shuffled to his bedroom. "It's fluids, right?"

"Not the same."

"Tomato, toe-mah-to," Carter grumbled as he crawled into bed. "Tap water, urine. Same diff." He made a show of organizing himself under the covers, then looked expectantly at Will. "I showed you mine. Now it's your turn."

"Fair enough," Will said and repeated his story of what happened the night before.

"So romantic," Carter said with a sigh. "What happens now? Are you going to be a snow day whore and go knock on his patio door like a stray dog?"

"What? No! I couldn't look him in the eye after all this."

"Really? But he likes what you've written, or so it seems."

Will nodded. "Yeah. But it would be just too... I don't know, vulnerable?"

"Yeah, I get that. So what are you going to do?"

"I was thinking about going to the bar tonight and seeing him in concert."

Carter widened his eyes. "Yes! Do that. Oh my God, if you don't do that, I will drag myself out to North Dakota and do it myself."

"I'm in upstate New York," Will said with a laugh. "And you stay in bed and rest. I'll go. But..."

"But what? Don't make me fly out there to Boise."

"I'm not in... Never mind." Will took a breath and let it out. "I was hoping you'd help me pick out something to wear? You're really good at putting outfits together."

"Absolutely." Carter gave a firm nod. "Let's do this right now, before I pass out."

"Sure you're up to it?"

"Clock's ticking, William."

"Okay, okay," Will said and crossed the room to the double doors of the closet. "Be kind."

"I'll be as gentle as possible, but no guarantees. Put on your big boy panties and let's do this."

Chapter Eight

The heavy thump of the music seemed to highjack Will's heartbeat as he stood against the wall and looked around the Side-Eye. It was set inside a converted warehouse with a massive, crowded-as-fuck dance floor set between a stage at one end and a bar made of corrugated steel at the other. A deejay stood on the stage, wearing headphones and dancing in place behind a bunch of sound equipment. A majority of the men thrusting and gyrating on the dance floor had peeled off their shirts and tucked them into their pants, showing off sculpted torsos both smooth and hairy, all gleaming with sweat beneath the flashing lights. The whole place was soaked in pheromones and body sprays, and Will couldn't look away from the writing mass of bodies.

He had never been comfortable in dance bars. His weight and overall size along with his natural inability to move to any kind of rhythm made him feel like a plodding elephant moving through a herd of graceful gazelles. When he and Carter had been dating, Carter had often dragged Will to dance bars, a different one for each night of the week. After several failed attempts to get Will to relax on the dance floor and just move to the music, Carter had finally stopped cajoling him to dance. When Carter heard a song he liked, he simply shimmied his way out on the dance floor alone. That happened often because Carter pretty much ran on caffeine and dance music.

A sudden, almost painful longing to have Carter there flared hot inside him. Will adjusted the sleeves of the button-down shirt Carter had suggested he wear. Okay, *suggested* was much too tame. More like *demanded*. Will had only worn the shirt once before, and now he remembered why. It was an athletic-cut style, and he didn't quite have an athletic-cut-style body shape, and that made the sleeves pull up. He had really liked the vertical striped pattern and the soft, cotton material, but he wasn't sure it had been the best choice to wear that night. His arms felt a little trapped, and his armpits were already damp.

This had been a bad idea. What had he been thinking coming out to see Rex perform? He was too nervous and self-conscious; he should just leave. But when would he get another chance to see Rex perform live?

His phone buzzed, and he pulled it from his back pocket. It was a text from Carter, and it made Will grin in spite of his nerves.

Don't you dare leave that place without listening to at least one complete set. I don't care how uncomfortable you are. You stay where you are, leaning up against the wall and feeling sweaty and like you could never compare to all the other men there. You are an awesome man who is kind and funny (well, sometimes), and handsome, with a glorious cock and the moves of a sex god to go along with it. Not to mention you are helping Rex Garland write a Christmas song! So you stay put, bitch, and don't even think about ducking out of there like some kind of baby pants coward. But definitely check your fly. You don't want to look like too much of a slut. I love you. Don't you dare leave!

Will read the message over several times, his smile widening. Carter knew him well. Maybe a little too well. He surveyed the dancers again, letting his gaze linger on the glistening, muscular bodies. It couldn't hurt for him to stay and listen to Rex sing. All he had to do was stand right where he was and maybe have a beer or two. The roads had been clear for his drive to the bar, so he shouldn't have a problem getting back to the hotel.

He shook his head and wrote Carter back: *You busted me. I was about to zip out the door like a cartoon character. Lots of hot, sweaty dancing men here, so you'd fit right in. I think I've already pitted out my shirt. But I'll stay. This is what I've been looking forward to for a long time. Thanks for the support. I love you right back. And your cock is nice too.*

Carter's response was almost immediate: *Nice?!?!*

Will laughed and sent back a heart emoji. He didn't feel like he belonged there, but he felt a little better about it, and that's what mattered. Abandoning his spot against the wall, Will waited in line behind a group of handsome twenty-something men, all with their shirts off to display beautifully toned torsos. They all flirted with the bartender as they ordered mixed drinks, laughing and reaching across the bar to touch his bare chest and belly. Once they'd been served, they strutted off into the crowd, all without sparing Will a single glance. He stepped up to the bar and flashed the bartender a nervous smile before he ordered a light beer. He hated the taste of light beer, but he was too self-conscious about his weight to be seen there among the beautiful people drinking something with any more calories.

Once he'd paid and tipped the bartender, Will discovered his spot against the wall had been taken. He wasn't really surprised. Lots of men liked to hang back and watch the sexy parade of flesh pass by. The bar area was pretty well lit, however, and it made him feel conspicuous and vulnerable. He merged into the flow of foot traffic heading back to the dance floor area and the safety of the shadows. A waist-high railing marked the borders of the dance floor, and Will lucked into an open spot close to the stage. He drank his beer and watched the dancers, marveling at their sinuous movements.

The music volume slowly dimmed until it had faded out completely. Will turned toward the stage, watching as the deejay pushed his equipment off to one side. The deejay picked up a microphone and slid his headphones off his ears and down around his neck as he walked to center stage.

"Hello Side-Eyers! How are you all feeling tonight?"

The crowd screamed in response, and Will laughed.

"Sounds like you feel good, but do you want to feel even better?"

More screaming, much louder this time, and the men pressed closer to the stage.

The deejay laughed this time, and a quiver of excitement ran through Will. Without even thinking about it, he had placed himself in the perfect position to be able to see Rex.

"All right, then, I guess I'll let you bitches get what's coming to you," the deejay said, and more screams erupted. "Give a big, boisterous, bitch-tastic welcome to our hot resident singer this month, Rex Garland!"

Will had no idea how the crowd managed to out-scream themselves, but they did. Rex strode out on the stage, looking good in a pair of tight black chinos and a white shirt with the top three buttons open to display his furry chest. As Rex waved to the cheering crowd, a black curtain parted behind him, revealing a woman sitting behind a drum set, a bass player, a guitarist, and a keyboard on wheels that a stagehand pushed forward. Rex moved behind the keyboard and played a few notes, the familiar opening of his first big hit, "Clean Slate."

The crowd shrieked with glee, Will included, but Rex stopped playing and leaned in close to the microphone and said, "What? Did you guys recognize those notes or something?"

Wild cheers and applause as Rex grinned.

"Well, maybe I'll play something like that later, but for now, how about something a little more upbeat for my Rexaroos?"

The drummer counted the band in by hitting her sticks together. Then they launched into the fun, bass-heavy song "That's Gonna Leave a Mark." Will sang along, lost in his study of Rex's expressions. Only about thirty feet separated them, so much closer than how he usually saw Rex back at the hotel. The times they'd talked in the hotel breakfast nook and at the rib joint, Will had been too overwhelmed by Rex's singular focus to process anything beyond simple facial recognition. Now, safely removed by being part of a crowd, Will couldn't stop staring. At least not until Rex looked right at him, locking his gaze with Will's as they both sang the lyrics. Heat rushed to Will's face, and he forced himself to turn away from that intense gaze. He looked instead to the dance floor where some guys were moving to the music, but most were singing along with Rex, just like he'd been doing.

None of them, he would bet, were helping Rex write a Christmas song.

Will worked up enough courage to turn his attention back to the stage and was both relieved and disappointed when he discovered Rex had looked away from him. Rex finished the song, and the crowd went wild. Will whistled, shouted, and applauded along with them, his smile widening further as Rex launched right into "Your Wicked Kiss," one of Will's favorites.

A whistle sounded from the dance floor, especially high-pitched and piercing. Will cringed and looked over his shoulder. A shiver of dread went through him at the sight of Andrew, his prima donna coworker. Oh shit, what was Andrew doing there? And with his shirt off, of course, because he had maybe three percent body fat and apparently all the motivation in the world to work out on a regular basis.

The urge to flee swelled inside Will. He wanted to snake his way through the crowd to the door at the other end of the bar, get in his car, and drive back to the hotel. Not because he was afraid of being outed—he didn't care about that. It was more trying to save himself from embarrassment due to his size. Andrew and the men gathered around him looked like perfect specimen of the male form, while Will... well, he did not. He assessed the crowd, gauging his chances of being able to make it through, and decided to just wait it out. If he tried to make it to the door now, he'd probably just end up drawing Andrew's attention.

Rex was deep into his set list now—something Will knew because he'd searched for it online—and Will was determined to enjoy the last few songs. He was impressed how good Rex sounded in person. It wasn't a surprise since he'd been listening to Rex sing in the courtyard, but he was still impressed. Some singers needed a lot of studio help to sound good.

Once Rex finished, he bowed to massive applause, waved to include his band members, bowed once more, and then dashed off backstage. The deejay reappeared almost immediately and kicked off more loud dance music. Will didn't want whatever the deejay was playing to minimize Rex's live performance, so he threaded a path through the crowd and away from the dance floor.

There was no sign of Andrew around the bar, so Will stood in line for another beer. He was at the end of the bar farthest from the entrance. Men talked excitedly about Rex and his songs or about the guy they met on the dance floor or the jackass who hadn't called back. Will tuned it all out and thought about Rex, wondering whether the men around him would believe him if he told them he had been helping Rex co-write a song.

A shout went up from the crowd as Will moved up in line. He turned away from the bar to see what all the commotion was and stopped dead, his heart pounding and his breath stuck in his throat. Rex had come out a door near the bar and was talking and laughing as men gathered around him. Will was trapped by the crowd with no place to go. Rex slowly worked his way through the men, shaking hands, posing for selfies, thanking everyone for coming out to support him.

Will realized that Rex was on a line that would bring him right to his spot. He looked side to side for a way to escape, but men were packed in tight around him; there was no place for him to go. When Rex was a few feet away, someone shoved past Will and the men around him, pushing his way forward in order to stand front and center before Rex. Will realized the rude, pushy man was Andrew and scowled at the back of his head. What a shithead.

"Hey guys!" Rex shouted over the music. "Thanks for coming out and braving the snow on such a cold-as-fuck night."

The men, Will included, laughed, but Andrew threw back his head and released a high-pitched chattering laugh that made everyone flinch. Including, Will was pleased to see, Rex.

Andrew put a hand on Rex's shoulder and said, "Oh, Rex! You're not only talented, but you're funny!"

Rex managed to keep his smile in place as he casually slid out from under Andrew's hand. "Oh, thanks. I really appreciate you coming out."

"Can I get a selfie?" Andrew held his phone up and smiled brightly. "Please?"

"Yeah, sure."

Rex stepped close, and Andrew put an arm around him as he brought his phone up. The crowd shifted a bit, and Will saw through a gap between some of the men that Andrew had his hand planted firmly on Rex's ass. And he also saw Rex reach back and move Andrew's hand off his ass and move it up to his lower back.

Will smiled, but it was short-lived when Andrew turned his head quick to kiss Rex's cheek right as he snapped the picture. What the fuck?

To his credit, Rex reacted better than Will would have. He stepped away from Andrew and planted a hand in the center of Andrew's chest to keep him at a distance.

"Not cool, man," Rex said. "Selfies are one thing, but that could be considered assault."

Andrew pouted. "It was just a sweet little kiss."

"Read up on consent, dude," Rex said. "Not cool. Don't do it again."

Several men immediately surrounding them murmured agreement. Andrew spun on his heel and forced his way out of the crowd in a huff.

Will's attention was on Andrew pushing his way through the men so he didn't realize Rex was right in front of him until the singer spoke.

"Hey! You're staying at my hotel, right?" Rex said.

A blank screen of static replaced Will's brain, and he just stood and stared into Rex's face with a stupid smile.

"And I saw you at the rib place, right?"

Words returned, but apparently only the words he had just heard spoken because Will said, "Rib place. Right."

"Yeah!" Rex grabbed his hand and shook it. "And you've got a spy name, right? Sorry, I can't remember it right now."

"Will." His name felt like a foreign word he didn't know the meaning of.

"That's it. Will. Will Johnson, right?"

Will nodded, trying to find a balance between the fact that Rex was still holding onto his hand, had recognized him, and remembered his last name. What the hell was going on? Had he slipped on ice leaving the bar and hit his head? Was he really back at the hotel, sound asleep and dreaming all of this?

"Thanks for coming all the way up here, man," Rex said. "I really appreciate it."

"I'm a huge fan," Will said.

Rex's smile softened but didn't completely vanish, and his eyes widened. Will felt Rex's fingers tighten a bit more as he continued to hold his hand.

"Oh yeah?" Rex said. "Are you a longtime fan?"

Will nodded. "Absolutely! Ever since your first song."

Rex leaned in and, still holding Will's hand, gently pulled him forward. Panic burst into supernova life in the center of his chest as Rex moved closer, crossing the personal space line and then continuing to close the distance between them. It felt as if sweat practically gushed from every pore as Will leaned back, trying to compensate for Rex's nearness. What the hell was happening? Was Rex going to kiss him? What the fuck would happen after that? And how bad was his breath after the beers he'd downed?

But Rex had no interest in kissing him. He was just leaning in close enough to whisper, "I caught you, my songwriting elf."

Oh shit! Oh hell-shit-fuck, Will had given himself away. And right there in the middle of the Side-Eye bar and surrounded by a pack of gorgeous men.

Will smiled and tried to look confused, but his expression felt more like terror than puzzlement.

"What?" A nervous laugh bubbled out, high-pitched enough to summon any nearby hyenas. "I don't know what... What?"

Will tried to tug his hand free of Rex's grip, but to no avail. Rex stood close to him, so close Will thought his face probably looked like a magnified pale round mask of surprise and dread. He pulled a little harder in an effort to break free but suddenly stopped. All sound and activity around them faded away until all Will could see and hear was Rex looking him dead in the eye and softly singing the lyrics to the song they'd written together.

One stocking hangs by the fireplace
But I'm lonelier by far on this Christmas
    Eve
You're so far away, so far from reach
My heart aches for you
But my mind still believes
You'll come back to me
You'll come stay with me

All the spit in Will's mouth evaporated, leaving him unable to speak. The only thing he could manage to do was stand there and stare. His head felt light and wobbly, as if he might just float up to the ceiling of the bar if he wasn't tethered in place by Rex's hand.

Rex's hand! He was still holding tight to Will, keeping him in place. The skin of Rex's palm was soft and warm, and Will hated that he was mucking it up with his big sweaty mitt.

"Rex!"

The shouted name broke whatever bubble had formed around them. Rex blinked and leaned back, but not before Will caught a flash of his happily surprised expression. What the hell was all that about?

Earl appeared at Rex's side. "Rex, come on. You need to get ready for your second set."

"Huh?"

Rex turned toward his manager, and once his gaze shifted, Will was able to slip his hand free and take a step back. A layer of sweat from head to toe left him feeling greasy. He used the back of his hand to wipe sweat from his forehead and took another step back.

Earl looked at Will, then back at Rex. "Everything okay? You look out of it."

Will decided it was probably a good time for him to slip away. He took a step to the side, his gaze locked on Rex as he and Earl continued to talk. A second step allowed another hot, muscular guy to move in front of him and block his view of Rex. Without Rex in his sight, Will was able to focus on retreating across the bar toward the exit. He'd left his coat in the car, and when he pushed out the door, the frigid night air immediately chilled his damp skin. Clutching his arms tight over his chest, Will threaded his way through the parking lot to his rental car, where he unlocked the door and quickly got inside.

He grabbed his coat off the passenger seat and pulled it on, gasping and shivering as the cold lining touched his already chilled skin. The engine turned over right away, and he cranked up the heat before driving out of the parking lot and heading back to the hotel.

What the fuck had just happened?

Chapter Nine

When he got back to his room, Will found a note stuck to the door.

Will—I got one of the techs to fix your heater. Should be good to go now. Doreen.

He took the note down and let himself into the room. The temperature was at a pleasant level, but what immediately caught his attention was the closed window with the drapes drawn tight. That was some powerful symbolism from the universe about how the evening had gone. No more secret serenades from Rex. No more helping with song lyrics. Time to put all of that childish daydreaming away.

He sighed and stripped out of his coat, tossing it onto the bed as he crossed to the window and pulled the drape aside. In the glow of the courtyard lamps, he could see the tiny snowman right where he'd left it on Rex's café table. Will turned away, letting the drapes fall back into place. It hurt too much to see the snowman and remember how excited he'd been when he'd first started dropping off song lyric notes. Carter had tried to ask him where his plan was going, but Will hadn't taken the warnings to heart.

And now look where he was.

He considered getting Carter on FaceTime, but his heart wasn't in it. He needed some time to himself, to wallow in his funk for a bit. He was still a little angry as well, at himself most of all, but also a little bit at Rex, even though he had no reason for it. Most of the anger was directed inward, mad at himself for not listening to Carter and not having enough foresight to realize what he was getting himself into. Did he really think Rex would want to date him? How would that even work? Will was a chubby office worker who lived in Boston, and Rex... well, Rex was pretty much the opposite of all that.

Opposites attract, a gentle, hopeful voice whispered in the back of his mind.

Will shook his head in a firm *no.* Not that opposite. There had to be some commonalities on which to build a foundation.

The song lyrics are your foundation.

The song lyrics were a joke, a passing fancy. They weren't enough to support anything but fantasies.

He unbuttoned his shirt and pulled it off, wincing as he caught a whiff of himself. Nervous flop sweat brushed with the bitter tang of adrenaline and terror. Maybe a shower would help wash not only the stink away, but his mood as well.

After a hot shower, he smelled better, but his mood hadn't improved. A sneeze snuck up on him as he crawled under the sheets, followed by three more in quick succession. He returned to the bathroom and blew his nose, surprised to find he was a little congested. Catching a cold would put the cherry on this shitty weekend, surprise day off from work or not. He carried the box of tissues with him as he returned to the bed and plunked it down on the nightstand.

Once he was settled under the covers, he reached for the TV remote but stopped when his phone buzzed with a text message alert. It was Carter.

How are things going? Tell me you didn't try to dance.

Despite his mood, Will managed a small smile. Deciding he might as well get it over with, he opened the FaceTime app and made the call. Carter picked up right away, his smile wide even though his eyes were watery and his nose red.

"So? Are you pregnant yet? Can I be the godfather?"

Will laughed and sneezed twice.

"Uh-oh," Carter said. "Did you have sex outside the bar and catch a cold?"

"No," Will said before blowing his nose. "I mean, I may have caught a cold, but it is definitely not from having sex outside."

"I'm sensing tension."

Will frowned. "You are?"

"I am." Carter nodded. "Even though I'm overcome by influenza and here in Boston and you're there in Nova Scotia—"

"Williamsville, New York."

"—I can tell you're not in a good place. What happened?"

Will hesitated but finally told Carter the story. He tried to repeat word for word the conversation he'd had with Rex, and at the end felt he'd done a fairly good job of it, even though his blood pressure had been through the roof and he'd been sweating buckets at the time.

"You outed yourself as the secret lyricist?" Carter said with a gasp.

"I outed myself," Will said. "And now I feel like an idiot."

"Why? He obviously liked your lyrics because he's been using them."

"Yeah, but look at the two of us."

Carter's eyes grew huge. "He's there with you now?"

"What? No! Why would you ask that?"

"Well, you said 'look at the two of us' like you wanted me to look at you as a couple."

Will frowned. "How much cough medicine have you taken?"

Carter grabbed the bottle from the nightstand beside him and squinted at the label. "The recommended amount, two tablespoons every... Oh." He set the bottle aside and smiled at Will. "Maybe a few tablespoons too much. But that's not important."

"Do not overdose on cough medicine, please," Will said. "I would never get over losing you."

"Aw, you're so sweet." Carter made a kissing face and smooching noises. "What would you miss most about me?"

"The way you always turn the conversation back to yourself," Will grumbled.

Carter frowned. Then understanding lit his face, and he nodded. "I see what you did there. Well done, Mr. Johnson, well done. So, back to you. What's the plan?"

"I don't know," Will said. "Wear a disguise whenever I'm in the lobby the next six days?"

"Six days? Is that when you're coming home?" Carter beamed. "I get my Big Willie back?"

Will couldn't help chuckling. "Yes, your Big Willie will be home on Friday."

"That makes me very happy, though I know I just turned things back to me again. Sorry," Carter said. "You don't think you could talk to Rex? Explain about the broken heater in your room and the open window and all of it?"

"I don't think I'd be able to speak to him at all. I mean, it's Rex Garland, for God's sake."

"Yeah, and, you know what?" Carter cocked an eyebrow and moved his phone closer so his face filled Will's display. "Rex Garland is a man, like you and me, and he's looking for someone he can be honest and true with. And I happen to know that there is no one more accepting and honest and true himself than you, my friend. I am so lucky to not only have had the pleasure of dating and sleeping with you, but being smart and persistent enough to make sure we remained friends afterwards. You've already given him a glimpse inside your heart with those romantic-as-fuck song lyrics. Give Rex a chance to see everything inside you, and he will be smitten for life. I guaran-fucking-tee it."

A tear rolled down Will's cheek, and he lifted his shoulder to dab it away before he reached for a tissue and blew his nose.

"Are you crying?" Carter asked in a gentle voice.

"No," Will stated firmly. "My cold is getting worse, and it's making my eyes water." He blew his nose. "Also, I might be crying just a little bit."

He took a breath and glanced at the drapes covering the window. All of his internal organs seemed to be trembling, as if they had been placed on a paint shaker set to low speed. After a moment to collect himself, Will looked back at his phone and smiled.

"That is the absolute most wonderful thing anyone has ever said to me. Thank you."

"You're very welcome," Carter said. "And I meant every word."

"You mean everything to me, too," Will said.

"That's very sweet, but it's not necessary," Carter said. "Let's focus on you and what to do about Rex."

"You know, I appreciate it, but I'm pretty tired. I think right now I need to turn out the light and go to sleep."

"Isn't it early for you there in Boise?"

"Upstate New York," Will said in a flat tone, but with a smile.

"Right, right." Carter smiled gently. "I love you, Big Willie."

"Love you right back, Cartier."

"Load up on vitamin C, okay?"

"You too."

"I'm hoping I'm on the downslope of this illness," Carter said with a dramatic sigh. "My Grindr profile is getting a bit dusty."

"Get some sleep," Will said. "Grindr will still be there."

"Yeah, I hope so."

Once he'd ended the connection, Will set his phone aside and turned out the light. He lay in the dark, sniffling and looking at the razor-thin line of light leaking in through the heavy drapes. Just a few more days and he would be back in Boston in his own apartment and with Carter and his other friends.

And away from Rex Garland.

❋

WILL'S COLD SEEMED TO MUTATE OVERNIGHT, AND HE STAYED in bed all day Saturday. The only time he got up was to open the door for Doreen when she knocked.

"Holy hell, what happened to you?" she asked.

"I'm sick," Will said, his voice coming out stuffy due to his congestion.

"All right, step out of the way." She waved him aside and grabbed fresh sheets from her cart before stepping into his room.

"I'm really not up to company," Will muttered, hand on the door handle as he watched Doreen stride past.

"You won't know I'm here," Doreen said. "Go brush your teeth and use the bathroom. I'll have your sheets changed in a jiffy."

"I don't have the energy to brush my—" Will stopped mid-sentence as Doreen fixed him with a steely look.

"Believe me, you need to brush your teeth," she said, then turned to fling open the heavy blackout drapes and let in the weak winter sunlight. She looked over her shoulder. "I did good getting your heater fixed, right?"

Will smiled sadly and nodded. "Yeah. You did. Thank you."

She frowned. "You don't have to look so sad about it."

"Oh, sorry. It's just... never mind."

He stepped into the bathroom and closed the door. One look

at his reflection made him wince. He needed a hell of a lot more than a tooth brushing.

It took him twice as long as usual to make himself even halfway presentable because he had to stop every few minutes and catch his breath. When he finally left the bathroom, Doreen had finished with the bed and was stacking clean towels on her arms.

"Thank you," Will said.

"Okay for me to go in there and clean up?" she asked, nodding toward the bathroom.

"Yeah, sure."

Will took a few steps toward the bed, then stopped when he saw the sheer curtains move a bit. He felt the cold air and, even through his clogged nasal passages, could smell the fresh scent of snow.

"I opened the window a bit to air the room out," Doreen said as she moved into the bathroom. "It was smelling a bit funky in here."

"Um, yeah, sure."

Will moved to the window and looked down into the courtyard. His snowman was still in place on the café table, but there was no sign of Rex. It felt as if something heavy and cold had been placed on Will's chest. He pressed his forehead to the glass and sighed.

"You don't like the snowman?"

Will jumped and turned to find that Doreen had come up behind him and peered over his shoulder.

"I like it fine," Will said, then followed that up with, "I should. I built it."

"Oh yeah?" Doreen moved to stand beside him for a better look. "Is that what you did the night I saw you trying to get out there?"

"Yeah." Will realized he had probably said too much and

turned away from the window. "It was just a silly thing I thought of. It doesn't mean anything."

"Isn't that the room where that singer is staying?"

Will stopped halfway back to the bed and looked over his shoulder. "You know about him?"

"Oh, sure." Doreen nodded, keeping her back to him. "My daughter likes his music. He's a nice man, too. Going to make some lucky man happy some day."

Will's brain was moving too slow to follow all the turns in his conversation with Doreen. He sat on the edge of the mattress and fixed his gaze on the center of her back.

"Have you met him?" Will asked.

"Rex?" Doreen turned to face him. "I have. I clean his side of the first floor as well as all the rooms up here on three. Do you know him?"

"We've spoken in passing, that's all." Will shifted his gaze away from Doreen's intense stare.

"Yesterday he was asking me all sorts of questions about other guests in the hotel," Doreen said. "Wondered if I knew of any songwriters staying here." She slid the window shut before facing Will again. "Have you ever written any songs?"

"What? Me?" Will blew a raspberry and shook his head. "No. I'm not a songwriter."

His heart pounded, and his cheeks burned. He couldn't look at Doreen, so he shifted his gaze to different spots all around the room.

"You're a snowman builder, though," Doreen said.

"What? Oh, yeah, I guess so. But that was just, you know, for fun. It didn't mean anything. How could I have known that was Rex Garland's room?"

"I don't remember saying his last name, so you must know who he is," Doreen said.

Will stumbled over his words as a feeling of defensiveness

surged within him. "Is this some kind of Agatha Christie play or something? Yeah, I know Rex's music. He's a very good singer and songwriter. It doesn't mean I wrote him secret song lyrics or anything."

"Okay." Doreen adjusted the sheer curtains a bit before approaching him. "Do you need anything?"

Will shook his head and managed to meet Doreen's eyes for half a second. That was long enough to see that she'd put it all together and knew what he'd been up to. He busied himself with turning down the covers and fluffing up the pillows, avoiding her gaze and hoping she'd just leave his room.

"No thanks, I'm fine. I appreciate the fresh sheets and towels. And sorry if I sounded snappish just now. I'm tired and don't feel well."

"No problem. You rest," Doreen said as she headed for the door. "Café down the block has good soup if you get an appetite."

"I'll remember that." Will climbed into bed and pulled the covers over him. "Thanks again."

Doreen paused at the door to look at him, then shifted her gaze to the curtains over the window.

"Sleep well," Doreen said before she left the room and pulled the door shut behind her.

Will lay beneath the covers and stared up at the ceiling. He let out a breath and shook his head, feeling static build up in his hair from the pillowcase. That hadn't gone very well at all. He'd pretty much outed himself as Rex's secret songwriter to two people now: Rex himself and Doreen, who apparently knew and talked to Rex every day.

"Just a few more days," Will whispered. "Not much longer."

❆

In the afternoon, Will worked up enough energy to take a shower. While it felt good to be clean, he was exhausted afterwards and got back in bed, falling asleep almost immediately.

His mind spun vivid dreams, most featuring Rex in one way or another. When Will woke again, it was evening, and the only illumination was the light from the courtyard lamps. He fumbled his phone off the nightstand and saw it was seven fifteen. His stomach rumbled, and he thought some soup from the café Doreen had mentioned sounded good.

Getting dressed took a lot of effort, and he had to stop and catch his breath a couple of times. When he was finally ready, Will left his room and leaned against the wall as he waited for the elevator. Once he'd reached the lobby, the sound of Rex's voice brought him to a stop the minute he stepped through the elevator doors.

"Look, is there any way I can get some kind of information about him?" Rex asked.

"I'm sorry, sir, but I can't give out any information about other guests," a young woman replied. "No matter what the intention might be."

"Even if I promise and cross my heart I'm not a serial killer looking for a victim?" Rex had turned on the charm, and from his tone of voice, Will could practically see his dimples.

"Even then," the woman replied with a smile in her voice. "I'm keeping your name and room number a secret, so it's only fair I do the same for every other guest."

"Oh? Has someone been asking about me?"

Will eased up to the corner of the elevator alcove and peered around it. Rex was at the front desk, elbows on it and his chin in a palm. The young woman only had eyes for Rex—Will couldn't blame her for that—so he had a short window in which to escape.

Trying to be fast and quiet, Will left the elevator alcove and headed for the hotel's main door, keeping his gaze on the floor and pretending to scratch the side of his head to hide his profile. With his eyes on the floor, Will didn't see the man before him until he heard him call out to Rex.

"Hey, Rex, we've gotta go. Come on!"

It was Rex's manager, Earl, and Will quickly spun and stepped around him with a mumbled, "Excuse me," before he darted outside. The wind was up, and the cold snatched his breath away. He didn't have time to react and adjust; he needed to keep moving. Will pulled his hood up, shoved his hands into his coat pockets, and trudged away from the hotel.

After walking half a block, he risked a look back. No one followed or stood outside the hotel looking after him. He'd gotten past Rex and Earl both. This time. Will let out a breath that clouded in front of his face. He just needed to do that for the next six days. No pressure.

He stopped and looked around to get his bearings. The diner was in the other direction, and Will set off for it, hoping the soup was as good as Doreen had promised.

Chapter Ten

After Sunday spent mostly in bed, Will felt much better Monday morning. He showered and dressed without having to stop and catch his breath or once staring wistfully at the closed window. Considering that progress on all fronts, physical as well as emotional, he gathered his things and left the room.

When he arrived in the lobby, he eased up to the corner of the elevator alcove and peered around it. From his vantage point, he could just make out the back of Rex's head where he stood in line for the breakfast buffet. Will's stomach rumbled impatiently, and he placed a hand over it and smiled briefly at a woman who stepped out of the elevator behind him.

"Waiting for someone," he said, trying to act casual but thinking he sounded more like a stalker. "Ride to work," he tried to add, but the woman had already hurried on.

It was a really good thing he would be leaving the hotel at the end of the week.

Pulling his hood up, Will kept his gaze fixed on the door and hurried through the lobby. It had snowed during the night, and he used the side of his arm to brush it off all the car windows, afraid the whole time Rex would come outside and call to him. He managed to clear off enough snow to be able to drive and got into the car, shivering as cold air blew from the vents.

And he was even more hungry now.

He stopped at a fast food drive-through for coffee and a breakfast sandwich and ate it during the drive. It didn't satisfy like the breakfast at the hotel, but it quieted his rumbling stomach.

Once he arrived at the office and removed his coat and turned on his computer, Will turned and was startled to find Andrew standing close behind him.

"Crap, Andrew, you scared me," Will said, feeling his blush return as he thought about seeing Andrew at the bar. Dammit, he'd been so worried about Rex; he hadn't had time to think about how to handle Andrew.

"Did you enjoy the show?" Andrew pursed his lips and narrowed his eyes. "I never would have taken you for a Rex Garland fan." He looked Will up and down. "Or someone gay."

Indignance pushed aside nervousness and stepped to the front of Will's brain. Because of his size and his preferred style of simple and comfortable clothes, Will had been treated like a secondhand gay ever since he'd come out. Every visit to a gay bar felt like being picked last for teams in gym. Carter's friendship had helped instill a touch of confidence over the years in Will's badly bruised ego, and it was this well he drew from as he straightened up to his full height and looked down into Andrew's pinched and pale face.

"Um, wow, there was a lot of inappropriate stuff packed into that," Will said. "I suggest you run statements like that through a mental filter first, unless you'd like to pay a visit to Human Resources with me."

Andrew's eyes widened, and slashes of crimson spread across his cheeks, making Will feel a warm sense of gratification.

"No, I didn't mean anything by that," Andrew stuttered. "I

was just surprised to see you at the bar. I had no idea you were gay, that's all. You looked like you were enjoying the music, so I just wanted to see what you thought."

"I liked it," Will said with a cool smile he hoped hid the nervousness building inside. What would Andrew think of his conversation with Rex afterwards? What was he going to say about that long of an interaction?

"Okay, I'll let you get to work then," Andrew said with a quick nod.

"Thanks for stopping by," Will said. "I do have a lot to get to before I leave at the end of the week."

"Yeah, right, okay." Andrew managed a quick, humorless smile before turning on his heel and walking off.

Will stood by his desk a moment, savoring the glow from standing up to Andrew as well as the relief that, apparently, Andrew hadn't witnessed Will's conversation with Rex after Rex had told Andrew off. That was more of a relief than Will had anticipated, so, with his mood boosted, he hummed his and Rex's Christmas song all the way to the break room to get coffee.

Chapter Eleven

On Thursday evening, Will said goodbye to the people in the office, even Andrew, and stopped in the office of the team leader, Bridget, on his way out the door.

"I fly out tomorrow morning," Will said. "Thanks for the information you provided while I've been here."

"Oh, ugh, you're flying out on Christmas Eve? I hope it's not a madhouse," Bridget said. "Thank you for all the help. You got us back on track and ready to work in the new year." She got up from her desk and handed him a red greeting card envelope. "This is a little token of my appreciation."

"Thanks very much," Will said and tucked the card into his messenger bag. "Give me a call if you have questions about any of the work I did."

"I'm sure everything will be fine. What time is your flight tomorrow?"

"Eleven thirty."

Bridget made a face. "I'll keep my fingers crossed for you. Another storm is predicted for tomorrow morning."

Will nodded. "I saw that on the news. I intend to leave the hotel extra early and light a couple of candles to the travel gods."

"Good idea. Safe travels home."

He shook her hand and waved to a few more people before walking out into the cold. He could smell snow in the air, and it made him shiver as he zipped his coat tighter. While he was more than ready to be home, he would miss Williamsville. Not just because of Rex and the secret song lyrics, but Doreen and the funky little Williamsville Inn as well. His room had been claustrophobic at times, but it had provided him one of the most romantic adventures of his life.

Unfortunately, all adventures had to come to an end, and many of them did not wrap up happily ever after. Even if Will never got the chance to have a coherent conversation with Rex, or even— God, it made his stomach hurt just to think about it—go on a date with him, Will had the memory of the song they'd sort of written together. And hopefully, once Rex released his Christmas album next year, Will would be able to listen to his contribution on repeat.

When he arrived at the hotel, Will hurried through the lobby, just in case Rex or Earl was hanging around. He took the elevator up to his floor, considering whether or not he should pack before or after deciding on dinner. Stepping out into the hallway, he was surprised to see Doreen's cart parked outside his room and the door propped open. He slid past her cart and into the room to find her hanging up fresh towels.

"You're working late," Will said.

"Yeah, one of the other girls quit this morning, so I'm doing twice the rooms." She smiled at him over her shoulder. "I saved your room for last, hoping I'd get to say goodbye."

"That was nice of you."

He hung his coat in the closet and started taking shirts off the hangers and laying them on the bed.

"I bet you're ready to be home, aren't you?" Doreen had come out of the bathroom and started helping by taking shirts off hangers and handing them to him.

"Yeah, I miss my own bed," Will said, then couldn't help glancing toward the window. "But I will miss this place." He smiled at Doreen. "And you, of course. Thanks for taking such good care of me."

"My pleasure," Doreen said, then gestured toward the window. "Have you talked with him yet?"

Will felt a nervous tremble in his belly and decided to act innocent. "Him who?"

"Don't play dumb," Doreen said with a shake of her head. "That Rex Garland whose patio you can see from your window. The guy who's been having trouble writing a Christmas song for a new album until some secret songwriting elf helped him out with lyrics."

All words and the power of speech fled Will's brain, leaving him standing and staring at her. Doreen crossed her arms and looked very pleased with herself.

"Guess I hit the bullseye," she said. "Don't think I've seen you at a loss for words all these weeks."

Will recovered enough to let out a nervous-sounding laugh and shake his head as he shrugged. "What? Bullseye? I'm just not sure what you're talking about."

"You're a bad liar, Will." Doreen approached and stood a few feet away. "Take it from someone who never took the chance she should have. Go talk to him. He's trying to find out who you are and what room you're in. He really wants to talk with you."

"You didn't tell him my room number, did you?" Will blurted.

Doreen smiled slyly. "So there's something to it then?"

Will sat on the edge of the mattress. "Dammit, Doreen, this isn't funny."

Doreen sat beside him. "I know it's not. But you have to

realize when you're standing at a fork in the road. What you decide to do today will have an impact on everything going forward."

"Well, that's no pressure at all," Will said, surprised to find he was fighting back tears.

"Take the time to think it through carefully." Doreen said. "Make sure you're at peace with whatever you decide to do because you will need to live with it for the rest of your life."

Will huffed quietly. "Do you give all guests here this kind of talk?"

"Nope, just the special ones." She patted his knee and got to her feet with a groan. "I'm glad this day is done, that's for sure." She turned to look down at him. "It's been good getting to know you, Will. I hope we get to see each other again in the future."

Despite his racing thoughts and pounding heart, Will managed to give her a smile. "I hope so, too. Thanks for taking such good care of me. You made my stay here a lot more special."

"You have the power to make it even more so," she said and gestured toward the window again. "Take charge of your life."

Will watched Doreen walk out the door and pull it shut behind her. What the hell just happened?

❄

WILL FINISHED PACKING MOMENTS BEFORE HIS PHONE LIT up with a FaceTime call from Carter. He smiled and accepted it, glad to see Carter looked much better since the last time they'd talked.

"It feels like you've been gone for fifteen years," Carter said in lieu of a greeting. "I am ridiculously excited that you're flying home tomorrow. When can I see you in person? I need a bear hug from my beary good friend." He smiled, showing his dimples. "See what I did there?"

Will laughed. "I do see what you did there, and it was very cute. I'm looking forward to seeing you too. I only hope I'll be able to leave tomorrow."

Carter's eyes widened. "Wait, what? You may have to stay? That's not fair! I demand more notice than this! Unless..." His expression and tone softened. "It's because of a certain singer-songwriter we both know and one of us loves with the fiery passion of a thousand volcanoes?"

"No no, it's nothing like that," Will said. "There's another storm predicted for tomorrow. I'm hoping my flight is early enough to miss it."

"Oh. Okay. So no further traction on this singer attraction?" Carter gasped and smiled. "I'm a poet and I didn't even know it! Hey, you think I could write songs for Rex too?"

Will nodded. "Sure, of course. Just get yourself assigned to a hotel room with a broken heating unit across a snow-covered and lamp-lit courtyard from Rex's room. No problem."

"My gay drama senses are tingling," Carter said. "What's happened since you talked to Rex at the bar?"

"Nothing," Will said with a sigh. "I've been dodging him and his manager the whole week."

"Dodging him? That makes it sound like he's been looking for you."

"Oh, I don't know about that," Will said, even though he knew precisely that was what had been going on, based on the conversation he'd overheard Rex having with the front desk clerk and what Doreen had told him. He had ratted himself out on the whole situation, which was yet another reason he would be glad to get back to Boston and his own apartment. No more sneaking around a hotel lobby and telling people half-truths.

Carter, of course, saw through the lie and called him on it. "I think you're lying. Tell me right now what's going on."

"Can it wait until we see each other? I'll be home tomorrow."

"Yeah, you'll be here, and Rex will be wherever he's got a gig scheduled next," Carter said. "This is your last night to make a difference."

"Do you clean hotel rooms as well?" Will grumbled.

"I don't know what that means, but I'm sure it wasn't meant to be hurtful." Carter fixed him with a pointed look. "Right?"

"No, it wasn't meant to be hurtful," Will said. "You sounded a lot like Doreen, that's all."

"She's the smart and caring hotel housekeeper you've mentioned?"

"Right."

"And she's called you out on this situation?"

"Right again," Will said.

Carter preened. "I can't think of a better compliment. Thank you. Now, talk to me."

Will explained how he'd been avoiding Rex and his manager in the hotel lobby. He added what he'd said to Andrew and the nice things Bridget had said. That reminded him of the card she'd given him, and he propped the phone up on the dresser to be able to pull the card from his messenger bag.

"What's that?" Carter asked.

Will pulled the card from the envelope. It was a hand-drawn scene showing a forest of pine trees covered in snow, the smallest tree decorated with tiny multicolored lights. He held it up to show Carter.

"That's pretty. Is that from Rex?" Carter asked.

"No, it's from Bridget, who I reported to here." Will opened the card and found a 250 dollar gift card for Amazon inside, along with a handwritten thank you note. "Nice little bonus for what I did here." Will held up the gift card for Carter to see. "250 bucks at Amazon."

"That is nice," Carter said. "It will buy a lot of Rex Garland's music."

Will tossed the gift card onto the bed and looked at the phone. "I can't do it, Carter."

Carter's expression softened. "Why not, Big Willie?"

"Because I am just that, okay? I'm Big Willie, and he's Rex the hot and talented musician. I mean, what the hell is he going to say?"

"I don't know. Maybe something like you're handsome and kind and write amazingly romantic song lyrics? Why do you have to try to predict everything that's going to happen?"

"If I don't try to predict it, I just end up getting hurt," Will said. "Over and over again."

"But that's no way to live your life," Carter said. "You need to step up and take a chance, or you might never get another shot."

"It's ridiculous, okay? He's all, you know…" Will waved his hands around as he tried to come up with a fitting description. "I don't know, he's all Rex Garland, and I'm… well, I'm me."

"Yeah, you're amazing and kind and handsome and loyal and generous and patient and funny and humble and sexy and really good in bed. What could possibly come of that?"

"You have to say stuff like that because we dated."

Will picked up the phone and sat on the bed. He felt tired and nervous and uncertain about everything. The past week he'd been focusing so hard on avoiding Rex, he hadn't given much thought at all to approaching him. He looked at Carter and smiled. "Look, I'll be home tomorrow. Can we save the pep talks and advice for then?"

"All right, I can see you're getting tired, so I'll let it go after I say one more thing. You'll be here in Boston tomorrow, but where will Rex be? Don't waste this chance, Big Willie. I really think you made a connection with him."

"Yeah, I'll think about it."

They talked about other things a bit longer. Then Will told Carter he needed to go out and find something to eat. Carter promised to make him a home-cooked meal once he got settled at home, and Will smiled. "Deal."

Will felt a sharp jab of loneliness once he'd disconnected the FaceTime call. He had a lot on his mind and no idea what to do and very little confidence to go with it. Doreen had been right about one thing; this last night in Williamsville did feel like a turning point in his life. He just didn't know which fork in the road he was going to take: the safe and familiar one, or the one that felt foreign and scary.

Maybe it was best left alone for now. Rex would be performing in his final show at the Side-Eye tonight. Tomorrow was Christmas Eve, and they would both be heading off home for the holidays. On Christmas Day, Will planned to drive to his parents' house in Hartford, and Rex would probably be visiting his mother where she lived in Palm Springs, on the opposite side of the country. There would be no surprise Christmas gift from Rex for Will. That kind of thing only happened in the movies, and this was Will's all-too-real life.

Well, all too real except for the secret songwriting he'd done.

With a small smile, Will grabbed his coat and headed out for his last dinner in Williamsville. Since Rex was performing at the Side-Eye, Will felt safe enough from discovery to enjoy a final meal at the rib joint. He lucked into the same table he'd had when he'd talked with Rex. The food tasted extra good that night, and he savored the tangy barbeque sauce and tender meat. He really needed to find a rib place back home he and Carter could go to. The thought of Carter deep-throating each rib bone to get the meat off made him chuckle, so he took a picture of his plate of food and sent it Carter with a note: *Do you like ribs?*

Carter wrote back shortly: *Does a bear shit in the woods? My Grindr date just showed up. You suck on a rib bone while I suck on his bone.*

"Incorrigible," Will muttered and shook his head.

Once he left the restaurant, the cold air felt good, so Will walked around a few blocks before returning to the hotel and going back up to his room. When he opened his door, he gasped at the heat that enveloped him and quickly took off his coat as he stomped across the room to the heating and cooling unit. It seemed to be set correctly, but the room's temperature was even hotter than it had been upon his arrival weeks ago.

Will pulled open the slider window and stepped up close to the screen, taking deep breaths of the refreshing air. He tried not to look down at Rex's little patio, but his gaze dropped there as if with a mind of its own. The snowman he'd built was still on the table, but Rex had added a tiny Santa hat. Will smiled and laughed, then shook his head and stepped back from the window.

No, it wouldn't work. He would be crazy to even open himself up to something like that. Rex was on a path to stardom and would meet thousands of hot, available men all over the world. And while Will himself was available, he was not exactly in the hot category.

He turned away and headed for the bathroom, putting Rex and all the songwriting foolishness he'd inspired in Will to the back of his mind.

❄

SOMETHING WOKE WILL FROM A DEAD SLEEP. NO, NOT something, but rather some*one*. It was someone singing, and it pulled him out of sleep like a siren song.

> *One stocking hangs by the fireplace*
> *But I'm lonelier by far on this Christmas Eve*
> *You're so far away, so far from reach,*
> *My heart aches for you*

But my mind still believes
You'll come back to me
You'll come stay with me
Weatherman says we're bound to get snow
But my heart's not feeling that holiday
   glow
Without you by my side
This Christmastime
Can I pretend you're mine for Christmas?
Can I wish for you this Christmas Eve?
All I want from Santa is your kisses,
Can I pretend you're mine for Christmas?
The lights on my tree
Don't shine quite as bright
Without you here beside me
Holding onto me tight
Since you've been gone
I've built a snowman all alone
And gone sledding on my own
All I do is cry and moan
Wishing for you to come back home
Can I pretend you're mine for Christmas?
Can I wish for you this Christmas Eve?
All I want from Santa is your kisses
Can I pretend you're mine for Christmas?
Can I kiss you underneath my mistletoe?
Can I tell everyone that you're my beau?
Can I pretend you're mine for Christmas?
Can I wish for you this Christmas Eve?
All I want from Santa is your kisses
Can I pretend you're mine for Christmas?

   The quiet strum of the guitar faded away into the night, and

Will lay very still, hands tightly gripping the covers he'd pulled up under his chin. He stared at the sheer curtains, glowing in the soft lamplight from the courtyard as a gentle breeze puffed them out.

Rex had finished their song. And he'd sung it out in the courtyard, just for Will.

"That's for you, Will Will Johnson, my secret lyricist," Rex said. "I wish I knew where you were staying so I could sing it for you in person." He was silent a moment, then huffed a quiet laugh and said, "Anyway, merry Christmas. I hope we meet again some day."

Will's brain screamed at him to stand up, to rush to the window and throw the curtains aside and call down to Rex. His brain wanted him to shout out his room number and invite Rex into the room and see what might happen next.

But Will remained in bed, muscles locked up and gaze on the gently billowing curtains. He had no idea what might happen after Rex got to his room—most likely nothing—but he couldn't risk embarrassing himself any further in front of someone as handsome and talented as Rex. That was something Will didn't think he could ever pull himself back from.

He forced himself to roll over, turning his back to the window and closing his eyes. Sleep, however, wasn't ready for him, and all he could do was run Rex's song on a loop in his mind as he stared at the wall. Tomorrow was Christmas Eve, and he was going to try and get back home just like millions of other people. What could possibly go wrong?

Chapter Twelve

"Delayed again! How long this time?"

The woman's annoyed voice drilled into Will's sleep-deprived brain, and he winced before pulling his carry-on bag a few more feet away. The woman's voice had been getting louder and sharper with each delay. Will couldn't blame her. He was frustrated as well, but he wasn't going to take it out on the desk agent or annoy everyone around him. One glance outside—yep, still snowing hard—provided reason enough for the delays. There was nothing any of them could do about the weather.

"I'm not sure, ma'am," the desk agent replied with more patience than Will thought he'd be able to muster under the same circumstances. "This storm has hit all over New York state and much of the eastern seaboard."

Will checked his phone and decided now would be a perfect time for some lunch. And maybe a drink or two. He sent a text to his parents to let them know he might not be able to make it home in time for Christmas, then another text to Carter about a further delay of his flight.

How many delays is that now? Carter wrote back.

Three, Will typed out. *And I'm sure there are more to come. Time to start drinking, I'd say.*

I'm heading that way now, Will wrote out.

Safe travels, Big Willie. So glad you're coming home.

Will smiled and typed: *Yeah, me too.*

But was he really that happy about it? He considered what had transpired during his time in Williamsville and had to admit it was kind of crazy. And romantic. A hell of a lot of romance. It was a memory he would always hold dear, and he hoped he'd be able to recall how it had felt to write lyrics and leave notes for Rex. Maybe someday he'd feel that kind of spark again, but for someone more readily available.

He chose a pub and lucked into a small table by the window. The waitress was an older woman, her hair a soft white cloud upon which she'd pinned a tiny Santa hat.

"Flight delayed?" she asked as a greeting.

"Twice so far," Will said.

She waved toward the window. "Might be a couple more yet, with this weather."

"Yeah," Will said. "I just hope Rudolph can show Santa the way."

"Too bad he can't show your plane the way, huh?"

Will laughed, then ordered a Guinness and a burger and fries. His waitress—JoAnn, according to her nametag—walked off, checking on her other tables on the way to putting in his order. He looked out the window and watched the steady snowfall. Speakers in the ceiling quietly played Christmas music, but none of the lyrics stuck with Will even though he knew each song very well. All he could hear was Rex playing his guitar and singing in the snow-covered courtyard the night before. Singing just for Will.

"Here's your beer, love," JoAnn said, setting his Guinness before him as well as a plastic cup of ice water. "Food will be up in a jiff."

"Thanks."

The beer was foaming and chilled the perfect temperature. He licked the foam off his mustache and turned his attention back to the snow outside. A new Christmas song started overhead—"All I Want for Christmas Is You," one of Will's favorites, but sung by someone other than Mariah Carey—but even that couldn't push out Rex's song.

That morning he'd packed up the last of his things and left the 250 dollar Amazon gift card on a pillow for Doreen along with a note wishing her a merry Christmas. He'd checked out at the front desk but skipped the breakfast buffet in order to leave early for the airport. Once he'd hit the highway, he'd found the roads so slippery he decided to get to the airport first and eat second. Unfortunately, eating had taken a backseat to checking his luggage, getting through security, and waiting through each delay. With his stomach running on empty, the Guinness made quick work and sent a wave of calm through him. He was so relaxed he sat back in his chair and hummed Rex's song as he looked out at the snowy scene.

Will was lost in his own world and Rex's lyrics, so he didn't realize someone was listening to him until that person quietly sang the chorus.

> *Can I pretend you're mine for Christmas?*
> *Can I wish for you this Christmas Eve?*
> *All I want from Santa is your kisses*
> *Can I pretend you're mine for Christmas?*

Will turned in his chair. Rex sat at the table behind him, brown eyes wide and bright as his smile.

"Will Will Johnson," Rex said. "As I live and breathe."

"Erp," was all Will managed to say in response.

"You're a tough man to track down. I think my first assumption was spot-on, and you are a spy. Did you hear me singing for you in the courtyard last night?"

Words had fled Will's mind, so he simply nodded. He realized his mouth was hanging open, so he closed it with a click of his teeth.

"Here's your burger and fries," JoAnn said, setting Will's food on the table. "Oh, do you two know each other?" Before Will could answer, JoAnn smiled at Rex. "You can move over here if you want, honey. Free up that table for someone else."

"Huh?" Will managed to say but was cut off by Rex's exuberant response.

"Thanks, JoAnn, I'd love that."

Before Will could really comprehend what was happening, Rex had taken the seat across from him. Will sat and stared at Rex Garland sitting on the other side of his small table. To his surprise, he saw Rex had a Guinness as well and a plate piled high with nachos.

"Good taste in beer," Rex said and held up his glass. "To song lyrics, snowstorms, and flight delays."

Will lifted his own beer and blinked when Rex touched their glasses together. He took a long drink as Rex did the same, both of them regarding each other. The beer seemed to lubricate the wheels in his brain because he heard words come out of his mouth.

"Your flight's delayed too?"

Rex nodded. "Yep. I'm trying to get to Boston to stay with my sister. How about you?"

Will's heart stuttered through a couple of beats. Had he heard Rex correctly?

"Boston?"

"Right," Rex said. "Boston. My sister lives there, and I travel so much I don't really have a base."

"Boston," Will said.

Rex casually slid Will's Guinness a little farther away from him and leaned in over the table. "You okay there?"

Will sat back in his chair. He looked Rex in the eye and took a long, slow breath. Maybe this was fate or luck or coincidence, but if he didn't do something right now, if he didn't take a step forward and grab the chance when Rex was sitting directly across from him, he would never be able to face himself in the mirror again.

It was now or never. He had to take a risk.

Also, if Carter found out he hadn't managed a coherent conversation with Rex, he'd never hear the end of it.

"It was me," Will said.

"What?"

"I left the song lyric notes."

Rex grinned and looked confused. "Yeah, I know. I busted you at The Side-Eye. I just didn't know what room you were staying in."

"327," Will said. "Directly across from your patio. My heating unit was stuck on Hellfire setting or something, and I had to keep the window open."

Rex sat back, and this time his smile was softer and not accompanied by a look of confusion. "That's how you heard me."

"I've been a fan for a long time," Will confessed. "I couldn't believe it when I heard you out there. When I realized you were having trouble with the song, I almost didn't drop off the lyrics. I mean, who am I to tell you how to write a song?"

"Everyone needs a little help now and then," Rex said. "Don't you think?"

Will thought about Carter, and Doreen, and, God bless her, even JoAnn the waitress, as he nodded.

"I travel a lot," Rex said. "Like, a lot. All of my stuff is either in boxes in my sister's basement or in a storage unit near my mom's condo in Palm Springs."

"You're not going to be with your mom for Christmas?" Will asked.

"She's got a new boyfriend, and they're going on a cruise," Rex said.

"That's too bad."

Rex shrugged. "It's all right. Palm Springs is nice, but I like having snow for Christmas. Although this…" He looked out the window, and Will did as well, both of them watching the blizzard in silence for a moment. "This is a little too much."

"Burger not done to your liking?"

Will looked up at JoAnn, who stood beside the table, her Santa hat at a jaunty angle.

"Oh, I totally forgot about it," Will said, blushing.

"Yeah," Rex added before he picked up a chip loaded with toppings. "Me too."

"Two more Guinness?" JoAnn asked.

Rex raised his eyebrows as he looked at Will. "What do you think? We've probably got about three hours to make our flight."

Will grinned. "Yeah, two more Guinness, please."

Once JoAnn left, he looked down at his burger and fries. He was hungry, but he felt really self-conscious eating in front of Rex. It suddenly looked like a lot of food, and Will was embarrassed at the huge burger between the two big buns as well as the heaping pile of fries.

"I really appreciate your help with the song," Rex said. "I haven't had much luck with dating lately. Too many losers or shallow guys who only want to be able to brag that they scored with me. Anyway, because of all that, I haven't really been in a romantic frame of mind, you know? At least, not until I started finding notes with lyrics from my longtime fan."

"Oh my God," Will said, face burning from a blush as he put his head in his hands. "I'm so sorry."

"Sorry? What for?"

"For all of it. I have no idea what I was thinking."

Rex tugged one of Will's hands away from his face and held it tight. "Look at me, Will."

Using every ounce of energy he had left, Will lifted his gaze and met Rex's eyes.

"What you did was sweet and caring and really kind. You nudged me out of my songwriting funk and gave me back hope that somewhere in this crazy, messed-up world, I might find a guy who was kind and funny and humble and genuine."

"You don't know me," Will said quietly. "And I'm so..."

"What? Handsome? Big enough to put my arms around and not feel like I'm going to break you in two? Strong enough to keep both feet on the ground even when you're in the middle of some whacked-out gay version of a Hallmark Christmas movie? And kind enough to the hotel housekeeper that she convinced me to stand out in the courtyard and sing to you even though I don't know what room you were staying in? Yeah, how do I know what kind of person you are?"

"Wait, Doreen told you to sing last night?"

Will tried to keep his brain from focusing solely on the fact that Rex still held his hand. His palm was starting to sweat, and he didn't think he could stand it if Rex let go of his hand and wiped his own palm on his jeans.

"Yeah. She caught me in the lobby as I was hanging around trying to catch you coming or going."

"You were trying to catch me?"

Will swallowed hard. Was this actually happening? Or had he been in an accident on the way to the airport, and this was all an elaborate coma dream?

"The hotel clerk wouldn't give out your room number. I guess I should put that in my Yelp review, huh? That plus one of the better breakfast buffets I've seen in a while."

"You were waiting for me?"

He couldn't get past the idea that Rex had been waiting in the lobby just to talk to him. How could that be? How had any of this actually happened?

"Hey, Will."

Rex squeezed his hand and tightened his grip a bit, as if trying to pull Will into the conversation. It worked, because Will suddenly found himself able to focus on Rex and what he was saying.

"I felt more of a connection with you through those lyrics than I have with any guy I've dated in the last couple of years. My manager warned me I was going to get into some legal shit if I used your lyrics, but I didn't think that was your angle."

Will shook his head. "It wasn't. I swear. I only wanted to help."

"Right. So I used your lyrics, and I think we wrote a pretty kick-ass Christmas song. Don't you?"

"Yeah, I do. I really loved hearing you sing it last night."

"That courtyard's got some great acoustics, I gotta say. So, come on, we've got a long wait ahead of us. Let's get over this 'I'm a singer and you're a guy who left me song lyrics to get me out of my funk.' Let's just be two guys who might have some kind of connection. What do you say?"

"Okay, that would be great. I mean, if you want. I'd like that."

Another squeeze of his hand. "So no more blanking out and staring at me?"

A fierce blush burned in Will's cheeks. "I don't know if I can promise that."

Rex laughed and released his hand. To Will's relief, he didn't wipe it on his jeans or even on his napkin. Instead, Rex used that hand to grab another chip loaded with toppings and stuff it in his mouth.

"I love to eat," Rex said as he crunched his food. He gestured to Will's plate. "Come on, don't let me sit here eating alone."

Will cut his burger in half and took a bite. It was perfect, and he looked away from Rex as he chewed.

"You never told me where you're flying to," Rex said, then laughed. "Or trying to fly to."

"Boston."

Rex's eyes went wide. "Are you kidding me?"

"Nope."

"You live in Boston?"

"Yeah, in South End."

Rex stared at him as a smile slowly lifted one corner of his mouth. "My sister lives in Back Bay. You might as well be neighbors."

"I didn't know that. Wow. And you're going to be there over Christmas?"

Rex had some more of his nachos, which encouraged Will to take another bite of his burger and sample some of the fries.

"Until just after New Year's," Rex said. "I'm doing a series of west coast shows starting in mid-January."

"Do you like traveling so much?"

Rex shrugged one shoulder. "It's been great to see so many different places, but it does get tiring. And lonely."

Will ate a few fries as he looked out at the snow. "I always thought you'd be surrounded by hot guys and had your pick of them."

"Well, as shallow as that makes me sound," Rex said. "It's not the case."

"Oh my God, I didn't mean that," Will said, that burning blush back now and even stronger than before. "I know you're not shallow. I'm sorry."

"I'm teasing you, Will, relax." Rex smiled and took a long draught of his beer.

"Okay, that's good. I'm really sorry."

"No need to apologize. I know the romanticized vision of life performing on the road. Hell, I dreamt about it all the time when I was growing up. But the reality of it is a lot different. Have I hooked up with some guys? Absolutely. Am I proud of that fact? Not really. I've always wanted someone permanent, you know? Someone to keep me grounded. Someone to share all the moments, big and small."

"Yeah, that does sound good."

Will was surprised to find he'd eaten half of his burger. He felt better and was able to focus more on the fact that he was sharing a meal and conversation with Rex.

"Have you written any other songs?" Rex asked.

"No. Never. I wrote some poetry in college, but it wasn't any good."

"I bet that's not true."

Will laughed. "Oh, it is. It was all angst-ridden stuff about being gay and someone who was bigger than most other guys."

It was out there now. Will had thrown the thing neither of them had touched on right into the center of the table. Now he would see how Rex reacted.

"I think you look great," Rex said. "Strong and husky and like a friendly bear. Your beard is amazing."

A half smile propped up one side of Will's mouth. "You like my beard?"

"Dude, your beard is sexy as hell," Rex said, leaning in over his nachos and lowering his voice. "It's thick and dark blond and looks soft and well-groomed. I've always liked stocky guys with full beards."

"Holy shit," Will whispered. "Is this real?"

Rex reached over and grabbed his hand again. "Will, this is real. Okay? Just sit back and relax, and let's get to know each other. Wait, you're going to Boston? What's your flight number? How crazy would it be if we were on the same damn flight?"

They each checked their phones and laughed when they saw

the same flight number. Rex sat back and stared at him. Will shifted uncomfortably. Finally, when he couldn't take it any longer, he leaned in over his plate and said in a low voice, "What?"

"We were destined to meet, Will Johnson," Rex said. "I feel it. You and me, we were brought together by the universe for some reason. I don't know if you believe in anything like that, but I do. There's an energy to the universe, you know? A power that helps bring people and events together. Sometimes it's for good, and sometimes it's for bad, but it's always out there. And it was working hard to get us together."

Rex waved a hand and made a face. "I know I sound like Yoda or something, talking like this, but I really believe it. Your room at the hotel with the broken heater, me staying right across from you with the little patio. That Christmas song I was dreading and you deciding to give me some help. Then we met in the breakfast line and at the rib joint and at my gig. Plus, Doreen stepped in to give us a nudge as well. We were supposed to meet. Don't you think so?"

Will nodded, eyes wide and staring at the beautiful man before him. "There have been a lot of coincidences."

"The universe, I'm telling you."

"Yeah. I could see it."

Rex finished his beer and lifted the second glass in a toast. Will looked down, surprised to find he'd finished his own beer and had a fresh one already waiting. When had JoAnn dropped that off? He lifted his glass and clinked it against Rex's.

"To snowstorms and song lyrics," Rex said.

"Hear, hear," Will said and took a long draught of his beer.

This might have been the best Christmas Eve ever.

Rex paid for lunch, joking that it was just a start of the royalties Will would earn for his share of the sales of their song. They wandered around the airport after that, talking about their childhoods and families, movies, books, and TV shows they liked, as well as favorite foods and vacation spots. Will was surprised with each similarity, but Rex just smiled and said, "That's the universe for you."

Back at their gate, Rex managed to get most of the other passengers waiting for their flight to sing Christmas carols, and Will was glad to see that even the harried employees joined in. At one point Rex sang their Christmas song and introduced Will as the song's co-writer, which produced a loud round of applause that made Will blush furiously and smile so wide his cheeks hurt.

Will hadn't thought at the beginning of the day that he'd ever think his flight boarded too soon, but after spending the hours in between with Rex, that was how it felt. Even though Rex had a first-class ticket, he stayed with Will and waited in line with him, both of them still talking and laughing. Once inside the plane, they parted ways, Rex going to first class and Will shuffling along the narrow aisle to his own window seat.

He smiled through the smooth takeoff, then looked up in surprise minutes after the seat belt sign went off to find Rex standing by his row. Rex offered his first-class seat to the woman in the middle seat next to Will, and she immediately got up and practically ran up the aisle. Rex dropped down into her seat, his knee pressing against Will's, and smiled at him.

"So, where were we?" Rex said.

Will thought his heart might explode right then and there. He sent a little prayer to God or the universe or whoever was in charge that he would live long enough to savor this interaction a little longer.

The plane landed in Boston what felt like minutes later, and Will and Rex took their time getting to baggage claim. In the past, Will had always hurried to baggage claim to grab his luggage and get the hell home, but now he practically strolled past the shops and eateries. Rex seemed to be in the same mindset, and Will had to convince himself again that this was all really happening.

Once they'd collected their luggage, they found a uniformed driver holding a sign with Rex's name on it. They followed the man outside to where a black Lincoln Continental waited at the curb.

"Did you park your car at the airport?" Rex asked.

Will shook his head. "I couldn't afford that many weeks of long-term parking."

Rex bowed and waved toward the car. "May I offer you passage to your homestead?"

"Why, thank you," Will said and handed his luggage off to the driver for stowing in the trunk. "But the way you said it makes me feel like I've about to head out on the Oregon Trail."

"You will not die of dysentery," Rex said as he allowed Will to climb first into the backseat. "At least not today. No idea what you get up to on your own time."

The drive from the airport to his apartment building had never gone so fast, and before Will realized it, he was stepping out of the car.

"Now I know your home address," Rex said with a smirk. "I've added it to room 327 at the Williamsville Inn in my mind."

"You remember my room number?" Will asked as the driver set his bags at his feet and discreetly returned to the car.

"I remember a lot about these last few weeks, Will Will Johnson," Rex said. He quietly sang, "Merry Christmas, darling," and leaned in to give Will a sweet kiss goodbye on the lips.

Will smiled stupidly as Rex got back into the car. He continued to smile as he watched the car move off down the dark, snow-covered street. His lips tingled, and his brain seemed stuck in a loop of screaming, *Rex Garland kissed me!*

Most definitely the best Christmas Eve in the holiday's history.

He laughed up into the snow falling from the dark, cloudy sky, then grabbed his bags and let himself into his apartment building.

Chapter Thirteen

Will's phone buzzed on the bathroom counter, and he glanced down at it, then smiled.

"Let me guess," Carter said. "It's from Rex."

Will pulled his attention from his phone and back to Carter's reflection in the bathroom mirror. Will stood behind him, reaching over his shoulders to work on tying Carter's festive bowtie. But he couldn't quell the smile from seeing Rex's name on his phone. "Yeah. It's from Rex."

"Where is he spending his Christmas Day?" Carter asked. "Some big fancy music industry party?"

"No. He's really not like that. He's got plans with his sister and her family," Will replied as he finished with the bowtie and stepped aside. "There. You're all set."

Carter assessed his appearance in the mirror. "You're the best. How the hell did you learn to tie a bowtie? I don't remember you going through a college professor phase."

"I missed that phase," Will said, picking up his phone. "I think it was more during my lack of dating and addiction to YouTube videos phase."

"That's funny, I thought you said YouTube and not Pornhub."

Will laughed but didn't look at Carter, focusing instead on Rex's text message: *Merry Christmas, Secret Songwriter. Thanks for making yesterday a Christmas Eve I'll always remember.*

"I don't think I've ever seen you smile like that," Carter said, cocking an eyebrow at him in the mirror. "Did he send you a dick pic? Show me!" He stepped up beside Will, wide eyes fixed on the screen of his phone.

Will laughed and held the phone to his chest as he walked out of the bathroom. "It's not a dick pic. I didn't meet him on Grindr, for God's sake."

In the living room, Will stood by the small artificial tree he'd setup before leaving on his trip and typed out a response: *Definitely one I'll never forget. I have to keep reminding myself it really happened.*

Carter stepped into the living room and assessed his tree. "I'm glad you already had your tree up, though it's not really up to snuff for the tree of a gay man. We'll work on that for next year. No trip to see your folks today?"

Will adjusted a handblown glass ornament. "I like my tree just fine, thank you. And no, no family visit today. I called them last night and told them what a crazy day of travel it had been, so we made plans for me to go see them next weekend."

"Smart. Think you'll get some more gifts because they'll miss seeing you?"

"Doubt it."

"Too bad." Carter looked at the tree once more. "So what are you going to do? Just hang out here by yourself all day?"

Will shrugged and nodded. "Yeah, sure. It's pretty nice, actually. I'm usually in a car driving over icy roads to visit my folks or something. Today I'm wearing pajama pants and a hoodie and eating whatever I want while watching whatever I want."

Carter pouted. "I want that now, too!"

Will laughed. "But you've got someplace to go, based on this bowtie."

"Yeah, some fancy brunch one of my Grindr regulars invited me to."

Will frowned. "You have Grindr regulars?"

"Well, you know, once you get familiar with the moves of one or six of them, it's pretty nice to be able to get a date whenever you're in the mood."

"I'll have to remember that."

"Do you really like your gift?" Carter asked.

"Boxers with obscene messages printed on them? I love them. You know I like to be secretly dirty around people. Did you like the ornament I got you?"

"A burly lumberjack with a beard and a big package? Absolutely." Carter smiled and waggled his eyebrows. "You are a secretly dirty person. I like knowing that about you while everyone else thinks you're the clean-cut, innocent guy."

"Looks can be deceiving."

"They certainly can." Carter studied him a moment. "It's nice to see you so happy."

"Thanks," Will said. "It's nice to feel this happy."

"That makes me feel good. Come here."

Carter pulled him into a strong hug. Will breathed in the subtle spritz of cologne mingling with the scent of Carter's shampoo as he returned the hug. Before he stepped back, he kissed the side of Carter's neck and said softly, "I love you, Cartier."

"I love you too, Big Willie."

They stepped apart just as Carter's phone buzzed. "And there's my ride."

"He's picking you up here?"

"Yeah. I Ubered over here and gave Mason your address."

"Hmm, thanks?" Will said.

"He's cute," Carter said as he headed for the door. "Once I'm done with him, you might want to try him on for size."

"I'm not the secondhand shop for your Grindr castoffs," Will said, trying to act insulted but unable to keep from laughing.

"Not when you've got the hottest gay singer in the country lighting up your phone and your gonads." Carter gave him a quick kiss on the cheek before hurrying out the door.

Once Carter had departed, Will started the water for a hot bath. While waiting for the tub to fill, he trimmed his beard and mustache and shaved the lower part of his neck and upper portions of his cheeks. He had to stop several times, though, because he kept wrinkling them as he smiled while thinking about the day before.

With his beard trimmed and cleaned up, Will got in the tub and thought about Rex as he soaked. When his fingertips wrinkled, he dried off, then dressed in sweats and headed for the kitchen, humming the song he and Rex had written together.

> *Can I pretend you're mine for Christmas?*
> *Can I wish for you this Christmas Eve?*
> *All I want from Santa is your kisses*
> *Can I pretend you're mine for Christmas?*

He slid a frozen macaroni and cheese dinner into the microwave and turned on the TV, selecting a mushy Hallmark Christmas movie. Once he'd settled in with his food and a beer, his phone buzzed, and Will smiled when he found another text from Rex.

Merry Christmas! How are your parents?

Will felt a thrill of excitement at the fact he was receiving another text from Rex Garland, then forced that thought aside. This was Rex, who wanted to be treated like any other guy Will might be interested in. So Will wrote him back: *I ditched my parents and have taken a hot bath and am eating a macaroni and cheese frozen dinner, drinking a beer, and watching a Hallmark Christmas movie.*

Rex wrote back almost immediately: *I don't know if I'm envious as hell or falling in love. Movie title, please.*

Will stared at the text a moment. Falling in love? What the hell? No. It was just a saying; it couldn't mean Rex was actually *in love* with Will. That was crazy. They'd just met. Like, literally just met the day before.

But you helped him write his song, a hopeful voice whispered. *That allowed him to get to know you as well.*

Gathering his thoughts, Will sent back the title of the movie and was surprised when a few minutes later Rex started texting him comments about what the actors were wearing and some of their lines. They exchanged funny comments for the rest of the movie, and once everything wrapped up sweetly, they sent the same text simultaneously.

Sigh!

Rex said he had to go eat dinner, and Will clutched his phone to his chest as he watched the beginning of another Christmas movie. Was this really happening? It was difficult to believe this was his life and not some gay Christmas romance movie. He tried not to get too excited about it all, but hearing from Rex on Christmas Day while the man was spending time with his sister and her family made Will feel as if Rex was invested in continuing whatever might have developed between them the day before. Or, actually, even further back than that.

Early into the next Christmas movie, the macaroni and cheese had its way with him, and Will dozed off with his phone on his chest. It buzzed an hour later, bringing him up from a deep sleep. He looked around in confusion, then remembered he was in his own apartment, and Rex had been texting him. Picking up his phone, he found two more messages from Rex.

Have you finished your dinner? Feel like some company?

Also, do you think this latest Hallmark couple are both wearing wigs?

Will snorted a laugh. Looking at the television, he decided Rex might be onto something.

He wrote back: *Definitely wigs. And I'd love some company. Who should I expect?*

While he waited on a response, Will pushed up from the couch and got busy picking up the place. He stacked the dirty dishes in the dishwasher, wiped down the countertops and sink, and then hurried down to the hall to his bedroom. Throwing open the double closet doors, he surveyed his clothes as a cold pit formed low in his belly. Denim and khakis. Why did he not own anything decent?

Will returned to the living room and picked up his phone. There was no response from Rex, and he tried to push down a strong sense of disappointment. Tendrils of the feeling snuck past his defenses, and as he headed back to his bedroom, phone in hand, Will's doubts fed off that disappointment and thrived. Had Rex come to his senses and decided he shouldn't see Will on Christmas Day? Had Rex's sister told him he was being crazy, acting so wrapped up in someone he'd just met? Or maybe Rex had heard from an old boyfriend and realized Will was just an average guy, overweight and stuck in a middle-class life.

To turn his mind away from his doubts, Will went through every article of clothing in his closet. In the very back, he found an outfit Carter had given him for Christmas the previous year. Carter was much braver in his fashion choices than Will and liked to buy clothes for Will he would never buy for himself. Will laid the outfit on the foot of his newly made bed and stepped back.

The pants were navy with a paisley pattern and made of wool. The button-down linen shirt was solid green. It was all tied together with a green-and-red plaid bowtie.

Will held the pants up against himself.

"I don't think I've ever worn any article of clothing made from wool and with paisley on it."

He checked his phone again—still no response from Rex—then stripped off his sweats and pulled on the paisley pants. They were a very tight fit, and he had to suck in his gut to get them fastened and zipped.

His hoodie went off next, and he pulled on the shirt. The linen was incredibly soft, but it was another athletic cut and felt tight around his belly. He shrugged into the shirt and fastened the buttons. It was kind of uncomfortable because it was tight, which the mac and cheese and beer contributed to. Minutes later, he'd knotted the bowtie and looked himself over. It was a nice outfit, but he liked wearing looser-fitting clothing.

He cleaned up the bathroom and made one more pass through the living room and kitchen. Everything seemed to be in order. Now he just needed to hold his breath for however long Rex stayed so he wouldn't risk splitting the seams of his clothes.

But what if he spends the night?

Will's stomach gurgled nervously at the thought. How the hell was he going to handle things if Rex wanted to have sex? There was no way Will could or wanted to turn him down, but he'd be a nervous wreck the entire time.

"Stop it," he scolded himself. "One thing at a time. Just enjoy hanging out with him. If he even shows up. How long ago did he send that text?"

Singing on the street outside started up as Will reached for his phone, and he paused. It was a man's voice, and he was playing guitar as well. Will smiled as he recognized the voice and the lyrics. It was Rex, standing outside his apartment and serenading him once again with their Christmas song.

Will opened the window and leaned out on the sill. Rex looked casual and handsome in his winter coat and bright orange stocking cap as he stood on the sidewalk, looking up at Will as he played guitar and sang.

There was so much Christmas romance wrapped up in that moment, Will thought his heart might explode.

Once Rex finished the song, Will clapped along with several people who had been walking by and who had stopped to listen. Rex laughed and bowed, then called up to Will, "It's better when I know which window is yours."

Will laughed. "I'm glad to hear that. Come on up. I'm on the third floor."

Rex arrived at Will's door, even more handsome than Will remembered. He stepped into the apartment and turned to look Will up and down, his eyes going wide as he took in the outfit.

"Damn, you look really nice," Rex said. "Did I interrupt you heading out? I can leave."

"No interruption. I'm staying home all day. I just—I don't know—felt like dressing festively, I guess."

Will shrugged and tried to keep his breathing under control. But it was difficult with Rex right there in his own apartment.

"Hell, my version of festive is this Christmas sweater and sweatpants." Rex took off his coat and held his arms out.

Will laughed as he took in the sweater depicting a scene from the ice planet in *The Empire Strikes Back* along with dark green sweatpants.

"You do look festive," Will said. "And comfortable." He put a hand on his belly and took a shallow breath. "I'm thinking I may follow your lead."

"Please do," Rex said, then lifted a six-pack of beer out of a paper grocery sack. "Care for a beer?"

"That sounds great. I'll be right back."

Will sighed with relief when he worked his way out of the shirt and pants. He hung them back in the closet, then selected a sweater with Yoda wearing a Santa hat and pulled on flannel house pants with a snowflake pattern. When he returned to the living room, he found Rex sitting on the couch watching the Christmas movie Will had left playing.

Rex smiled when he saw him. "Now you look comfortable. And festive. Oh my God, you have a *Star Wars* Christmas sweater too?" He pressed the back of his hand against his forehead. "I'm swooning."

Will sat on the opposite end of the couch and lifted the beer Rex had opened for him. It was cold and delicious, and he smiled nervously. He had no idea what to say or even how to begin a conversation. What had happened to him that Rex would even want to know about?

"Your folks must be missing you," Rex said.

Will shrugged. "Maybe. I think they were relieved as well. They worry about me driving there and back in one day, and now we can plan out a better time for me to visit."

"Still, I'm sure they miss you," Rex said. He put his head back and looked at him. "I know I did."

"What? No. How could you? We barely know each other." Will had to look away from those gorgeous eyes and take another drink of beer.

"I really like what I do know about you," Rex said and shifted a little closer on the couch. "I like it a lot. And I want to get to know even more about you."

"Not sure there's anything exciting enough to tell," Will said, hating the defeated tone in his voice but unable to stop it.

"Are you kidding me? You're wearing a *Star Wars* Christmas sweater, like me. You're living in Boston, and I will be too."

Will turned to look at him. "You will?"

"Yeah. I'll be staying with my sister and her family between tour dates."

"Oh. That's great. I mean, it's great you'll have a home base with family."

Rex smiled. "It is. And someone else here in town I want to get to know."

Will couldn't push back the strong surge of hope that rose inside him. "You do?"

"I really do. I haven't felt a connection like this with someone since my childhood best friend. I'd like to date you, if that would be okay with you. I'd like to see if this would work out given more time."

"I'd like that, too," Will said. "But it's hard to believe."

"Yeah, it's weird, I know," Rex said with a nod. "But I think we could make it work if we both really want it to."

"Okay, sure," Will said.

"And I didn't come over here for some Christmas Day booty call, either," Rex said, holding up his hands as if in surrender. "I only wanted to spend time with you, watching movies and hanging out. Let's see where things take us."

"Okay, sure," Will said, nodding back. "I was definitely not planning on sex since I ate mac and cheese and am drinking beer."

"Oh? Is there a food item or beverage I should keep an eye out for that could tip me off?"

Will laughed and blushed. "Well, it wouldn't be frozen dinners and beer that make me feel bloated."

Rex laughed as well and slid closer in order to take Will's hand. "Is it okay if I kiss you right now?"

Will's mouth went dry and he lost all power of speech. The sweet kiss the night before had been a surprise, and he hadn't gotten a chance to worry about it. Rex asking for consent was great, but Will's brain had time to run through a thousand different terrible scenarios before Rex's lips touched his.

The kiss started out soft and sweet but slid into something more heated and intense. Rex's tongue traced the line of Will's mouth, and Will opened to him. Fireworks and explosions and supernovas went off in Will's mind as they kissed, and when Rex finally pulled away, he was glassy-eyed and smiling.

"Damn," Rex whispered. "Tell me it felt as intense to you."

"Yeah," Will said, his voice catching and forcing him to clear his throat. "Yes. Absolutely."

"Good. Wow."

Rex leaned in for a series of sweet, shorter kisses, asking in between them, "Do you have plans on New Year's Eve?"

Will kissed him back, relishing the softness of Rex's lips and the feel of his talented tongue. "Not that I know of."

Rex kissed him once more, firmly, then held Will's face in his hands and looked him in the eye. "You do now."

Epilogue

Will pulled his rental car into a space in the parking lot of the Williamsville Inn and shut the engine off. He'd been smiling for at least a week now, ever since Rex had sent a plane ticket and rental car voucher via express mail to Will in Boston. It was Christmas Eve, and Rex had invited Will to return to the hotel where they'd first met.

The romance of it all made Will swoon. It sometimes felt as if he'd spent a majority of the past year swooning over something Rex did. He just hoped Rex swooned a bit himself from time to time.

Will got out of the car and grabbed his carry-on bag from the back seat. Walking into the hotel, he stopped and looked around the lobby. Some updates had been done to the decor, but the breakfast buffet area was still there, and a Christmas tree blinked serenely in a corner. All in all, it was very much the way it had looked when Will had checked out a year ago. Back then, he had been rushing through the lobby to avoid seeing Rex. Now, he was rushing to meet Rex. What a difference a year made.

Will approached the front desk and gave his name to the friendly girl waiting there.

"Here you go, Mr. Johnson," the clerk said. "You're in room 327."

Will laughed. "Oh my God."

She smiled nervously. "Is there a problem?"

"Nope. Everything is perfect." He took the keycard from her. "He thinks of everything. Thank you very much."

Will chuckled the entire ride up to the third floor in the elevator and continued as he made his way down the hall to the very familiar door of room 327. He let himself in and was very happy to see the room had been updated with more modern furnishings, including a memory foam mattress. There was a note on the pillow that made him smile: *Welcome back, Will! Enjoy your stay, and I'll see you soon. Merry Christmas, Doreen.*

The heat was set to a pleasant temperature, but Will slid the window open and looked down into the courtyard. The same small café tables and chairs on the same postage stamp patios, all of it buried beneath deep snow.

Rex wouldn't be arriving until later that afternoon, so Will unpacked and took a shower. After drying off, he wrapped a towel around his waist and stood before the full-length mirror in the entryway. He'd focused on working out more often and eating better the past year and had seen some good results because of it. It wasn't anything Rex had suggested he do; it was something Will had done on his own, for himself.

Will grinned as he thought about their sex life. The first time had been on New Year's Eve, and Will had been kind of self-conscious, but Rex had made him feel relaxed and confident.

"I'm a bear chaser," Rex had said with a casual shrug. "I like my men beefy and agile, and baby bear, you check both of those boxes. Just relax and enjoy it."

Rex's attentions had helped Will relax, and the first time had been great. Each time seemed to only get better, and Will had shared this with Carter, who immediately started saying "Sex with Rex" over and over. When Rex and Carter got together, there was no telling what would be said or sung, and Will had learned he just needed to sit back and let them go.

He got dressed and sat the desk, opening his work laptop. Still with the same company, he'd been promoted to a team leader role over the summer and was really enjoying it. He had a good team, and even though the manager he reported to was sometimes hard to read, Will liked her. A few emails were waiting in his inbox, so he replied to them. With the last email sent, Will made sure his out of office was set for the following week, then surfed the web and read some news.

Someone started playing guitar down in the courtyard, and Will sat back and laughed. He shut down his laptop and turned to the window, pushing the blinds aside and opening the window as far as possible.

Rex stood on the same patio he'd been at last year, but this time, he looked right at Will's window. The tune he played was very familiar. It was, of course, "Can I Pretend You're Mine for Christmas," the song they'd written together, the royalties for which Rex had offered to split with Will. But Will had asked for his share to be donated directly to an organization that provided food, shelter, and counseling for LGBTQ youth all across the country. If Will had found happiness by helping Rex write that song, he wanted to help other LGBTQ kids find that as well.

Will sang along, his breath clouding through the window screen. But Rex changed up the words when he came to the chorus, and Will frowned and stopped singing to listen to these updated lyrics. Instead of the actual lyrics that went,

> *Can I pretend you're mine for Christmas?*
> *Can I wish for you this Christmas Eve?*

> *All I want from Santa is your kisses*
> *Can I pretend you're mine for Christmas?*

Rex sang,

> *Will you always be mine for Christmas?*
> *Will you marry me this New Year's Eve?*
> *All I want from you is a yes*
> *Will you always be mine for Christmas?*

Tears flooded Will's eyes, and his heart pounded. Had he really heard Rex sing what he thought he'd heard? Will stared down at his boyfriend, whose voice he'd fallen in love with years before and now whose heart he'd apparently won. Rex continued singing all the original lyrics of the song, but when he reached the chorus, he sang the updated version once again:

> *Will you always be mine for Christmas?*
> *Will you marry me this New Year's Eve?*
> *All I want from you is a yes*
> *Will you always be mine for Christmas?*

Will laughed and clapped his hands. He turned in a circle, doing a little dance before shouting down into the courtyard, "Yes! Yes! Yes!"

Rex laughed and sprinted toward the door leading into the hotel, high-stepping through the deep snow. Will laughed as he watched him, then hurried to the room door to pull it open. He leaned in the doorway and watched the corner of the elevator alcove, his heart beating fast and his hands shaking.

The stairwell door opened at the end of the hall behind him, and Will turned to find Rex sprinting toward him, the guitar slung across his back. Rex was panting a bit, but it didn't stop him from grabbing Will in a tight hug and kissing him hard.

"Yes?" Rex asked when he pulled back.

Will nodded. "Yes. Always."

"I love you, Will Will Johnson."

"I love you, too, Rex Garland," Will said. "So much."

Rex kissed him again, slowly walking him back into the room and letting the door swing closed behind them.

THE END

More Williamsville Inn gay romance

The Cupid Crawl
by Hank Edwards

A hook-up app serial dater.
A Valentine's bar crawl.
A day that will change their lives.

Carter Walsh will be alone on Valentine's Day, and his plans include a candy sampler of hook-ups. But once he learns about the Cupid Crawl—a bar crawl covering a half dozen bars, both gay and straight—he decides on a change of plans.

At the first bar, Carter meets Harry, a divorced dad coming out later in life, and he's far from impressed. Harry's definitely not the type of guy Carter would ever swipe right for. But as the Cupid Crawl hops from bar to bar, the two seem to naturally gravitate toward each other, and before he realizes it, Carter's succumbed to the magic of Valentine's Day and ditched the hook-up app to spend all his time with Harry.

❄

The Cupid Crawl is a funny, sweet, and steamy opposites attract, divorced bi-sexual dad, slight age gap story that takes place in the Williamsville Inn series world, and features characters from the Christmas stories **Snowflakes and Song Lyrics** by Hank

Edwards and ***Snowstorms and Second Chances*** by Brigham Vaughn.

Get your copy of ***The Cupid Crawl*** today!
https://books2read.com/cupidcrawl

Snowstorms and Second Chances
by Brigham Vaughn

A hotel room with a faulty heater.
A holiday grump who's sure he's straight.
A single guy full of Christmas cheer.

Erik Josef is a recently divorced businessman with one goal: wrap up his last project of the year so he can spend the holidays in the tropics. While waiting at an airport bar, he encounters Seth Cobb, a chatty young travel writer.

After a huge snowstorm grounds all flights, a mix-up at the Williamsville Inn leads to them sharing a room.
Will a mugful of Seth's hot cocoa and the Christmas magic swirling amidst all the snow in upstate New York be enough to melt Erik's icy exterior?

❄

Snowstorms and Second Chances is a wintertime treat about forced proximity, self-discovery, and a second chance at happiness that takes place in the Williamsville Inn series world. It features characters from Brigham Vaughn's **The Cupcake Conundrum**, along with **Snowflakes and Song Lyrics** and **The Cupid Crawl** by Hank Edwards.

Check out Brigham Vaughn's <u>**Snowstorms and Second Chances**</u>.

https://books2read.com/SnowstormsandSecondChances

❄

The Cupcake Conundrum
by Brigham Vaughn

A pastry chef nursing a broken heart.
A single dad who made the biggest mistake of his life.
One guest room to sleep in.

When Adrian Cobb arrives in New York to help his brother move, he comes face to face with the worst decision he's ever made—ghosting on a baking conference hookup a year ago. Now, he's sharing a guest room with Ajay Sunagar, who looks as tasty as the pastries he bakes, and Adrian desperately wants to prove he can handle the heat this time.

But although the attraction's still there, Jay makes it clear he isn't ready to forgive and forget. As they spend more time together, Adrian begins to wonder if Jay would rather make him grovel or cover Adrian in frosting and lick him all over.

❄

The Cupcake Conundrum is a sweet-treat story about a single dad, instant attraction, and falling in love all over again that takes place in the Williamsville Inn series world. It features characters from Brigham Vaughn's **Snowstorms and Second Chances**, along with **Snowflakes and Song Lyrics** and **The Cupid Crawl** by Hank Edwards.

Treat yourself to Brigham Vaughn's **The Cupcake Conundrum**!

https://books2read.com/TheCupcakeConundrum

About the Author

Hank Edwards (he/him) has been writing gay fiction for more than twenty years. He has published over forty novels and novellas and dozens of short stories. His writing crosses many sub-genres, including contemporary romance, rom-com, paranormal, suspense, mystery, wacky comedy, and erotica. He has written a number of series such as the funny and spooky Critter Catchers, Old West historical horror of Venom Valley, suspenseful FBI and civilian Up to Trouble, and the erotic and funny Fluffers, Inc. Under the pen name R. G. Thomas, he has written a young adult urban fantasy gay romance series called The Town of Superstition. He was born and still lives in a northwest suburb of the Motor City, Detroit, Michigan.

For more information:
www.hankedwardsbooks.com
hankedwardsbooks@gmail.com
www.facebook.com/groups/hankshangout

Also by Hank Edwards

Critter Catchers Series

Terror by Moonlight

Chasing the Chupacabra

Swamped by Fear

The Devil of Pinesville

Screams of the Season

Horror at Hideaway Cove

Dread of Night

Critter Catchers Universe Stories

The Mystery of the Morelock Motel

Critter Catchers: Level Up Series

Grave Danger

Williamsville Inn Gay Romance:

Snowflakes and Song Lyrics

The Cupid Crawl

Fake Date Flip-Flop

Star-Spangled Showdown

Lacetown Murder Mysteries
(co-written with Deanna Wadsworth)

Murder Most Lovely

Murder Most Deserving

Venom Valley Series

Cowboys & Vampires

Stakes & Spurs

Blood & Stone

Up to Trouble Series

Holed Up

Shacked Up

Roughed Up

Choked Up

Fluffers, Inc. Series

Fluffers, Inc.

A Carnal Cruise

Vancouver Nights

Standalone Gay Romance

Buried Secrets

Destiny's Bastard

Hired Muscle

Plus Ones

Repossession is 9/10ths of the Law

Wicked Reflection

Holiday Gay Romance:

A Gift for Greg (A Story Orgy Single)

Mistletoe at Midnight (A Story Orgy Single)

The Christmas Accomplice

Story Orgy Singles Gay Romance:

A Gift for Greg

By the Book

Cross Country Foreplay

Mistletoe at Midnight

The Cheapskate: Bad Boyfriends

With This Ring

Gay Erotic Short Story Collections:

A Very Dirty Dozen

Another Very Dirty Dozen

A Third Very Dirty Dozen

A Fourth Very Dirty Dozen

Salacious Singles Gay Erotic Short Stories:

Bear Market

Convoy

Double Down

Exchange Rate

Finding North

Hotel Dick

Kindred Spirits

Sacked

Stroking Midnight

Vanity Loves Company

Wet Lands

CPSIA information can be obtained
at www.ICGtesting.com
Printed in the USA
LVHW101651190223
739892LV00001B/238

9 798570 954113